The Red Rider

JB Trepagnier

The Red Rider © 2020

All Rights Reserved. No part of this publication may be reproduced, stored in a retrieval system, or transmitted, in any form or by any means —by any electronic, mechanical, photocopying, recording, or otherwise, without prior written permission.

Cover by Hannah Stern-Jakob Designs

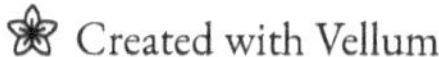 Created with Vellum

The Red Rider

The Horseman of War is on the scene, and nothing about the apocalypse prepared me for Dice.

I thought Aeron and his murdering horse were crazy. Try everything about Dice. I'll bet his murder horse is even worse than Aeron's. We've moved from Mexico to Dice's base in Florida. If you're wondering where all the military ended up after the war, they all follow the Horseman of War now. It must be his angel superpower because not only does he have planes and firepower here, he's got people that can use them. He's got people all over the freaking world.

I don't know the first thing about war. In fact, I slept through World War III. Dice has bombs ferreted away, but we aren't using them to light my father's ass up and send him back to Hell. The three Horsemen I've met so far have some long-term plans. So, Dice is fiddling with explosives to make them into a delivery device for Leif's zombie killing serum without blowing the rest of humanity to kingdom come.

Did I mention the part where we are letting a dude with a bright red mohawk and rainbow suspenders play with bombs? Because that part has me a little worried, and I've already been chased by zombies and dealt with five trucks full of Nazis.

To my family. Well, if you made it this far, Thanksgiving is officially going to be awkward. Did you download this because you're shooting for Christmas too? As if my gag gifts aren't enough. I guarantee this will be way worse than the time the wrong person got the farting animal coloring book in the pick a gift exchange.

Foreword

When He broke the second seal, I heard the second living creature saying, "Come." And another, a red horse, went out; and to him who sat on it, it was granted to take peace from Earth, and that men would slay one another; and a great sword was given to him.

ONE

Dice was still standing right up in my personal space with his wonderful smell and his shirtless chest. That toothpick was just lazily hanging out of his mouth. I needed him to get away from me. There was something about that deranged look in his eyes that was drawing me in, and I didn't know him. Plus, I was already dating two of the Four Horsemen, and I didn't need to start collecting them like Pokémon.

I pressed my hands against his chest and then remembered he was only wearing those rainbow suspenders up top. I jerked my hands away like he was on fire and eased myself away from him. Dice just chuckled and chewed on his toothpick.

"Is she always this skittish?"

I grabbed Smurfette off the table. I always kept her nearby, even in Leif's secure lab. I poked him in the chest with her.

"I don't know you, buddy."

"Once you've painted someone in an orgy, you're old friends. Did you get my cock right?"

"I swear to God, if you whip it out in this lab, you're taking my bat to your balls."

Dice just winked at me and turned back to Leif and Aeron.

"She's fun. When do we leave?"

"You're a little early, Dice. We talked about you coming later, but you insisted on coming now. I need to help with the vaccinations here."

Dice just rolled his eyes.

"You have people for that. I'll bet it bore poor Aeron senseless."

Aeron just shrugged.

"I've got a girl and a lot more fucking patience than you ever did."

You mean to tell me Dice had less patience than Aeron did? Why were Leif and Aeron giving Dice the stink eye for getting here early? Didn't we need him here? We could use all the help we could get.

Leif just rolled his eyes.

"Between the two of you, I don't want you breaking my shit. And Dice, no recruiting. We need the soldiers here, where they are."

"Oh, please. I can contain myself. You know I like to spread things out. I trained most of the older soldiers here and left them where they were, didn't I?"

"I haven't broken any of your shit since Ariel and I got here," Aeron pointed out.

"Yeah, but the two of you tend to feed off each other, and that's when my shit starts breaking."

Yeah, I could see that. War and Death went hand in hand, and shit tended to get destroyed in the process. Aeron could have a big stick up his ass when it came to my safety, but I'd also been around him when he let his hair down. I could see him acting up with Dice. I'd been staring at that fucking laptop for so long, I wouldn't mind causing some trouble that didn't upset Leif.

Aeron and Dice both snapped to attention and placed their hands over their hearts like really massive boy scouts.

"We solemnly swear not to break anything," they both said at the same time.

They were so not boy scouts, and I had a feeling they had said that numerous times since they were created and Antichrists started getting sent to Earth.

"That means nothing anymore," Leif huffed. "You say that every time and you always manage to break something of mine. Remember the Antonine Plague?"

"You're *still* mad about that?" Aeron asked.

Dice just popped his suspenders.

"We did kind of cause the end of the Roman Empire with that one, and the end of the Pax Romana meant I had to stick around longer. It's serious this time. Fine, Leif. We'll make a concerted effort not to break anything while we are here."

Aeron ran his fingers through his hair.

"Okay, I'll give you the Roman Empire, but you do know Dice is more effective when he breaks stuff, right?"

"When he's breaking Antichrist stuff. Not *my* stuff."

Dice gave his suspenders a hard pop again. His hazel eyes were trained on me, and he was smirking again.

"Maybe the pretty Nephilim should babysit us."

Leif just scowled.

"You're a full angel, Dice. You don't need a Nephilim babysitter."

"No, but I'd like one when they are that cute."

"Get out of my lab! You too, Aeron. Go kill something. We are so close to have things blow up in our faces now. We need to handle things here so we can leave for Florida."

Dice just slung an arm over my shoulder.

"I'm going to borrow your Nephilim. If her powers are starting to show and she's exploding things, then she needs to be taught how to harness it and control it. She can use it to defend herself when we take the White House and kill Isaiah."

Leif just sighed.

"Sorry, Ariel, but you aren't doing that in my lab, and you can't do it in public. Use my private chambers, but try to keep the shit breakage at a minimum."

"I don't want to break anything, Leif."

He touched my cheek.

"I know, Speedy. You need to learn. You're handy with Smurfette, but I'm not sure what you can do with that explosive power of yours. It could be a needed long-range weapon in your arsenal, and Dice is the best person to teach that."

I knew why I needed to learn this, and it would be nice to have a use for it other than power outages. Still, there was just something about being alone with Dice that made me nervous.

Two

Dice seemed to know his way around this lab, and no one seemed to bat an eye about a shirtless man with a mohawk leading a pink-haired girl covered in tattoos down the hallways. Did I mention how much I was loving Mexico? Even with all the gunfire and bombs going off on the other side of the wall, people were pretty chill.

I was less chill about Dice. He was just strolling next to me, whistling with that toothpick in his mouth and his hands in his suspenders. Why did he make me nervous? Probably because I knew he knew I had painted that scene in the White House. Did that make shit awkward? Because it felt awkward.

It was like someone who didn't know you existed finding your diary and reading all your weird sexual fantasies with them. Like you could ever live that down. If that ever happened, the only thing you could logically do was completely move states and delete all your social media for a while. I'd fucking painted us getting busy with all his angel friends in the Oval Office, and we'd never met before.

How fucking mortifying.

What do you even say when you meet the person in your painting for the first time? Why did this shit always seem to happen to me, anyway? At least I knew it had a name now. I was a Harbinger. Socially awkward shit aside, I did help Mexico stop invading Nazis, so maybe it wasn't totally horrible.

Dice knew the password to the keypad on Leif's room and let us in. He blocked the door and wouldn't let me in right away.

"Okay, Leif is really materialistic when he gets called and likes to surround himself with human comforts we can't get in Heaven. Given human comforts are pretty sparse right now, treat everything in his rooms like they can't be replaced. There's probably a long-ass, sentimental story about even the knickknacks on his coffee table. He hates it when things get destroyed because he's attached to all his possessions."

"I thought you were teaching me how *not* to destroy things. I knocked power out to the entire building."

"Do you want a congratulation? Only baby angels do that. I'll be so proud of you when you start shooting laser beams out your hands, little Nephilim."

Did the Horseman of War seriously just give me a noogie? He was going to mess up my hair. I shoved him away and stomped into the apartment. I pointed Smurfette at his head.

"*Never* do that again."

Dice just crossed his arms and smirked at me. Then, he jumped and practically shrieked. I jumped too because when the Horseman of War screams like a woman, something fucked up like a Rage Head mutant rat in the room was probably happening. Out of instinct, I jumped on the sofa and held Smurfette ready.

Dice wasn't in fight mode. He wasn't even screaming anymore. He was rifling through the trashcan like he was utterly insane. I stepped off the couch because clearly, there were no mutant rats in here. Dice was just excited about trash.

"Anything exciting in the garbage there, Tiger?"

"Never let anyone say I'm not considerate. I promised Leif we wouldn't break anything, but you need a target. I'm going to make you one."

"This is a bad idea. Why can't we wait until we get somewhere we can do this outside? Isn't there a place at your base in Florida we can work on this?"

Dice just snapped his suspenders again, then took his toothpick out his mouth and gave me a stern look.

"We're on a timeframe, cupcake. Do you think mastering divine powers like this is going to be easy? You need to start now, and we'll still be working on it in Florida too. Godly lasers. Do you think that shit is easy? I know you saw Aeron in action when those dumbasses came here in big trucks. You don't have the power to do all that, but don't you want to learn to defend yourself with it? Don't you want vengeance on your father? We'll help you get that, but you have to put in the work. I'd like nothing more than to see you hit him with a little angel magic, then beat the shit out of him. We aren't picky over who gets to kill the Antichrist as long as it gets done. We all think you should do it, except Asher, but he usually has his head up his ass."

Well, shit. That was the most double-sided motivational speech I'd ever heard. Most people didn't try to pump you up to kill your father. Well, I'm sure someone out there had this conversation at least once, but it was my first time.

It was so fucked up, but yeah, it had my blood pumping. I had the Four Horsemen of the Apocalypse, letting me kill the Antichrist. It probably would have gone a lot quicker if they did it, but they were totally on board with me bashing his face in with Smurfette. How cool was that?

"I just don't want to blow the power out so that it can't be brought back up."

Dice beamed at me.

"I've never met a power grid that hated me before. I will give you the Dice guarantee if you knock the power and the generator out, I will get it back up."

"But Leif has samples in the lab!"

"Different generator. Are you done complaining? Shit, girl, did Aeron have to give this big of a pep talk to get you out of that lab?"

I grabbed a pillow off the couch and threw it at him. He easily caught it and threw it back at me.

"Asshole."

"Yeah, but I'm an effective asshole. Look!" Dice said, holding up a target he made from trash.

He'd even managed to make a bullseye on it. How the fuck did he manage to do that while we were arguing. I crossed my arms. It was time for a little payback.

"Well, that's cute."

Dice was totally unflappable.

"I aim to please. Now, help me find a place to put this. Leif doesn't exactly have wall space free. How about the front door?"

Dice pulled chewing gum out his pocket. Where the

fuck was he finding gum during the apocalypse? He saw me looking at him.

"Florida is mine. I can take what I want."

"Leif is going to kill you," I said when he stuck his target on the wall with the gum.

"He'll understand. You're stalling. Go stand by the doorway to the bedroom."

Why was I so nervous about this? It was more than just breaking Leif's shit and a power outage. I'd seen the aftermath of Aeron using his angel powers. I didn't want to think I was capable of doing that, even if I really wanted to aim it at my father.

"Can I do what Aeron does with his?"

Dice just shrugged.

"You're uncharted territory. I've never trained a Nephilim before, but from what I understand, they can only cause the lights to flicker. You're a little more angel than they are. Anyone who looks on the true visage of an angel has kind of the same result as what you saw with Aeron. He just packs a little extra punch because he's the Horseman of Death."

"So, I could blow that door down and hurt someone."

"Wouldn't it be just the little bit badass if you could?"

"No!"

"Yes, it would. Now, go stand in the door and focus."

Dice came and stood behind me. I felt his arms wrap around my shoulders. He trailed his fingers down my arm until he grabbed my wrist. He lifted my arm and aimed my palm at his target. My heart was thudding in my chest. What was this man doing to me?

"Focus on what you felt when you exploded that light bulb, but try to harness it."

Easy for him to say. I was kind of in the middle of

getting laid. Like I remembered anything other than intense pleasure. I wasn't exactly feeling that right now. I was nervous as shit, and being in this close proximity to Dice's naked chest wasn't helping.

"What's wrong?"

"I was having sex when I made the light bulb explode, and the power go out."

"Do you want to have sex right now?"

"Asshole!"

"I was going to offer to get Aeron, Ariel. I hardly know you either."

"I don't fuck with an audience."

Except for that one time, but Dice didn't need to know that.

"Well, you need to do something, because you need to get your angel boner up."

I whirled around and bumped right into his chest. I stepped back because he shouldn't be allowed to smell that good.

"You just expect me to be able to do it. Maybe you should explain the mechanics first."

Nothing ever seemed to bother Dice. He just shrugged and took my arm to lead me over to the couch. He plopped on one end and stuck his big, head stomping boots in my lap like we were at that point in our relation-ship. I lifted his boot by the tip and removed it from my lap. Yeah, I was a little conflicted about the Horseman of War.

"It's tied to your emotions, yeah? We all use different things to access our angel grace. You need to look deep inside and figure out what your trigger is."

"Well, I'm certainly not going to be thinking about sex when I face my father."

"No, you're going to be pissed. But you can use that. It's not just one emotion. It's powerful emotions in general. I'll bet if you thought of him and tried again, you'd be able to call your grace. Forget blasting shit for now. Let's chat."

I cocked an eyebrow at him. I thought the whole point of pulling me away from Aeron and Leif was to teach me this. Yeah, it made me nervous as shit, but so did the idea of just having a chat with Dice. Why did this angel unnerve me so much?

"Talk about what?"

"Girl, you wake up from a coma and can't remember shit. You wake up in the middle of all *this,* and you find out Daddy is the Antichrist, and your mom was an angel. Aeron isn't huge on talking about feelings, and I imagine Leif has been buried in his test tubes since you got here. We've never met, but I've had to listen to those two goofy mother fuckers wax poetic about how even your farts smell good. Call me curious, and you probably need to talk to someone that doesn't think the sun shines out your ass."

"Aeron talks, and Leif isn't buried in his test tubes all the time."

"Call it professional curiosity. None of us have been up close and personal with Isaiah like you have. I've listened to his tantrums, but you know his weaknesses."

"Yeah, but I don't remember them."

Dice just smirked at me.

"Then, talk to me, and maybe we can jog your memories loose."

He was right. I needed to remember, and anything I could give them that would result in Isaiah's death would help. I hopped up.

"Have you had Maria's salsa? If we're chatting, I want food."

"That's the spirit! And yes, I've had her cooking. She cooks like she's heaven touched."

I wandered off to find Maria. I was going to remember if it killed me, damn it.

THREE

Dice was now shirtless and barefoot. He seemed to want to keep touching me with his feet. Angels must not have stinky, sweaty feet because it didn't bother me all that much. He seemed to enjoy eating just as much as I did. He was leaned back against the arm of the sofa with a bowl of salsa resting on his naked chest and his feet touching my thigh.

"So, out with it. How are you handling all this shit?"

"Is there an option not to handle it?"

"Sure. You could have said no to all this at any time. You could have stayed with your Nephilim friend in California."

I paused with a chip halfway to my mouth. It just kind of hit me right then.

"Do you and Asher know every little thing about me? I don't know a damned thing about you."

Dice just smiled at me.

"I only know what Aeron and Leif have told me. For instance, neither of them told me about the little noises you make when you eat. It's pretty hot. So, why didn't you stay with Mabel? You've known her longer, and you just had a steaming load of shit dumped in your lap."

"Well, yeah, but I'm not selfish. I did flip out when I kept drawing horses, but Aeron kept saying my blood held the cure. I didn't know about everything else then, but why would I doom humanity just because I had a little freak out?"

Dice narrowed his eyes at me.

"Plus, if word got out your blood had the cure, people would come for you."

My chip felt like a rock in my throat. I swallowed it down with some water. That thought hadn't even crossed my mind, despite how protective Aeron was with me. No, it wouldn't have gone down like that. Aeron wouldn't have.

"Aeron wouldn't have sold me out like that. You've known him longer than me, but I think you know this."

"No, he wouldn't have, but he also wouldn't have just left you in California. He would have stayed until he wore you down."

"He didn't have to, Dice. Where are you going with this conversation?"

Dice just shrugged.

"The truth. I know Leif and Aeron's version of the story. I also know they are in love with you and maybe telling me this story with rose-colored glasses."

"What do you want me to say, Dice? I lost my shit in Los Angeles, but I still came. Aeron didn't have to threaten me or kidnap me. Did you ever stop and think for a minute that I love them too?"

Oh, shit, did I just say that? Did I actually say the L word about my online boyfriends? I'd never said that about any of my boyfriends before, even if we didn't have some online thing going before we met. What were these angels doing to me?

Dice just winked at me and popped a tortilla chip in his mouth.

"And now we've reached the heart of the matter."

"Excuse me?"

"Aeron and Leif might as well be my brothers. Angels don't have siblings like humans do, but we were all created at the same time with one purpose. They are in love with you. Aeron was practically insane when I got called down here, and you'd already been missing for a few years. Leif wasn't much better, but I've never seen Aeron like that before."

I gaped at Dice.

"Are you having some angel version of the *don't hurt my brother* talk with me? Seriously, with everything going on, you're worried about me playing Aeron and Leif? There are fucking zombies out there, and we just got attacked by Nazis. Is this a whole *my dad is the Antichrist* thing? Because I'm nothing like him!"

Dice just laughed at me. *He fucking laughed at me.* If food wasn't scarce and I wasn't still hungry, he'd be wearing his guacamole I was eating. I was butt-ass pissed and offended. Did he seriously think I wasn't capable of caring for Leif and Aeron because of my father? Like it was going to be in my DNA to hurt them. I think I was pretty much at the point that I'd go just as crazy as everyone kept telling me Aeron did when I was kidnapped if anything happened to them.

"Is something funny, fucker?"

"I wasn't trying to be offensive, Ariel. I wasn't hinting you were anything like your father, either. The four of us are ancient. You're what, in your forties now? Aeron and

Leif are practically obsessed with you. While you were in that coma and dreaming, they had time to do nothing but worry about you and let their feelings grow. You just knew them online, and then you were forced to sleep. I wouldn't blame you if your feelings weren't as strong as theirs. It sounds like they are, though."

"And you had to piss me off to find that out?"

"I don't think you realized it until I challenged you, Speedy."

I snapped my mouth shut and pouted. He wasn't wrong, but I didn't like being poked and prodded into admitting my feelings. I tried seeing a therapist after I got settled after I ran. I don't think it was therapy in general, just the fact that the therapist I chose wanted me to deal with my shit on their time and not my own. I wasn't ready to confront all the shit my father put me through in two one-hour sessions and didn't go back. Miss Mabel was sort of my therapist. She let me talk about things in my own time, and I didn't have to try to get everything out in one specified hour.

"You're adorable when you pout."

"Oh, shut up!"

The door slid open, and Aeron and Leif came in. Leif noticed the target stuck to the door with chewing gum right away. Aeron zeroed in on Dice lounging on the couch with me.

"Seriously, Dice? Gum? I live here!"

"I thought you were supposed to be teaching her," Aeron grumped.

"She needed a target, and I *am* teaching her. You're all gung-ho to pit her against Isaiah, but you know just as well as I do, there's already going to be a lot of unresolved shit in the air when we get there. If you don't want her to destroy everything and not just Isaiah, we need to talk about everything we can."

Wait a minute, what? All I'd done was cause a power outage. I was pretty sure my father couldn't make me lose my shit to the point that I destroyed the entire white house. Plus, I would have four angels as backup.

Aeron just deflated.

"Yeah, I guess you're right."

"Use the spray adhesive next time. I don't want your spit all over my door. It's not sanitary."

"I'm an angel. My spit is divine."

"No gum on the door, Dice!"

"Fine! Ariel, welcome to *Dealing with Your Shit 101.* I'm your new therapist. I take payment in salsa and foot rubs."

I rolled my eyes. I guess this was really happening. The Horseman of War was my new therapist.

"I'm not touching your feet, Dice!"

Four

I would have thought our plan was finally coming together now that we had a cure, and Dice was here. Things just seemed to have gotten tenser. Leif kept snapping at Dice like he was going to trash his entire apartment, and Aeron was back to being grumpy again. We were all back in the apartment trying to eat dinner, and shit was just super awkward. No one was talking, and everyone was paying so much attention to their food, it was like they thought it could talk back.

I wasn't having this. If Dice were inserting himself as my new therapist, my unqualified ass would psychoanalyze their angel asses right back. If I was a loose cannon when we got to the White House because I hadn't dealt with my shit, what did they think was going to happen if we got there and they couldn't even have dinner together? And there was still some mysterious Horseman out there I hadn't met yet that I'd already been told didn't do team sports.

"What in the exact fuckity fuck is going on? I thought we would be celebrating Dice getting here and moving closer to stopping Isaiah. You all look fucking dire, and this meal is even more awkward than the time I let myself into Miss Mabel's apartment, and she was entertaining a gentleman friend on her couch."

"Ew," Aeron said.

I punched him in the arm.

"Watch it. Even old Nephilim need to get laid. She started hanging a sock on the door on the nights she had naked friends over."

"I think that's beautiful," Dice said. "If I actually aged, I would hope I was getting some right to the very end."

"Thank you," I said.

"Ass kisser," Aeron muttered.

I threw up my hands.

"What is your deal? You too, Leif. I get not wanting your stuff broken, and I'll admit the gum was gross, but you're both being a little mean to Dice."

"Yeah, the both of you are being mean to poor little me."

"You aren't helping!" I snapped.

"He's not supposed to be here!" Leif exploded.

"He was supposed to wait for us to come to him. He's supposed to be getting things ready for us to come to him!" Aeron snapped.

"Well, he's here now. Maybe he can help."

"He could help by going back to Florida and building delivery devices for my serum. That's what he needs to be working on."

"He's here flirting instead," Aeron said. "He's here because of that painting."

I nearly spit out my food. Out of everything I'd ever

painted, I think that was the one I regretted the most. If I could crawl under the table and die, I would have.

"Can we forget I ever painted that?"

"She said no, and she has the power to change it," Aeron said.

Hold up. Wasn't Aeron all gung-ho about the orgy? He seemed to be all on board with me banging his friends. Why was he getting pissed about it now that Dice was here? I finally just asked him about it.

"We need the Horseman of War on point. You don't know Dice when he gets distracted."

"Well, wouldn't he have just gotten distracted anyway when we got to Florida?"

I was so confused. Aeron and Leif made it seem like they wanted my painting to come true, and that meant me getting involved with Dice and Asher too. I wasn't even sure why I was defending Dice so hard if he was supposed to be working on a delivery method for the serum instead of being here with me.

I guess that was it. He knew what he was supposed to be doing. We all knew what he was supposed to be doing. All he knew about me was what Leif and Aeron told him. He risked pissing them off to teach me how to defend myself.

And he was right. I could puff my asshole out all day about bashing Isaiah's brains in with Smurfette, but I spent my entire childhood petrified of him. Scared enough to run all the way across the country to get away from him. I honestly had no idea how I would react when I saw him again. I could either go John Wayne and beat his face in, or I could lose my shit and get us all killed.

Yeah, I could appreciate Dice coming here to help me not get killed. I also didn't want to lose my shit in front of my new boyfriends. How embarrassing would that be? I'd lost my shit plenty of times, but I think daddy issues beat Nazis in terms of losing your shit.

"I'm *not* distracted. If you can get me parts, I can start working on a device while I teach Ariel."

"If you weren't distracted, you'd be in Florida," Aeron growled.

Dice finally lost his cool a little.

"Fuck you, Aeron. If I'd met Ariel first, fell in love with her, and couldn't stop talking about her, you'd be here too. Especially if you knew a fucking Harbinger painted all of us getting in on the love. You'd be here trying to figure shit out too. And I'm doing what you're trying to do too. I'm teaching her to defend herself. You know how Asher and I feel about this."

"Excuse me, how *does* Asher feel about this? Is he going to show up and try to make my painting come true too?"

Dice just grunted.

"Asher wants nothing to do with you and thinks we should drop you back with Mabel before we go to the White House. I'd feel better if you were with her too, but I get you need blood."

I turned to Aeron, who was one big pouty angel at the moment. Leif seemed to be tuning out the entire conversation and glowering at the gum on his door.

"It would be smarter if I stayed with Miss Mable while you went to the White House, but I can't. If I'm not the one to kill him, I need to see him die. If Dice can work and teach me, then I need his help because I don't know how I'll react when I see my father again."

"I'll have your back, Ariel. We all will."

"That's what I'm afraid of. I don't know the first

thing about summoning Satan, but you might have my back so hard, it gives Isaiah time to bring him into the mix."

Aeron was totally adorable when he knew I was right, but he hated it and didn't want to admit it. And I knew he was going to hate it even more when I pinched his nose gently.

"You know I'm right. Now, stop being cute and stick your lower lip back in."

Aeron huffed, but I could tell he wanted to smile. He had to keep up his asshole façade in front of Dice.

"Fine. I get it. But if Dice is going to stay here, he's sleeping on the couch. I'm not sleeping with his cold feet all over me again, and I'm not giving up my spot sleeping next to you."

"Is that settled? Can we stop growling and pouting now?" I asked.

Leif finally tore his eyes away from the chewing gum on the door.

"It's done. Let's watch a movie before bed. Dice, you are aware we don't have bombs here like you do in Florida, right?"

Dice just leaned back into the pillows.

"I'm just building parts. You do realize I have to convert nuclear bombs into devices that will release an aerosol and not blow shit up, right? It might take me ten minutes instead of five. I have to put it all into blueprints and get it to bases all across the country. I know the next words out of your mouth are that I should be in Florida playing with my bombs, but that's already what I've been doing. I've got a full fucking day, and I still have time to do my radio show. Now, what movie are we watching? Do you have any Mel Brooks?"

I expected an argument from the resident movie quoting geek, but he finally seemed to agree with Dice about something.

"I could go with some Mel Brooks too."

Leif just nodded.

"The one director we all agree one. I could scrounge up some Mel Brooks."

Aeron yanked me into his lap while Leif started rooting through his DVDs. Dice's eyes never left me. I wasn't mad they were finally getting along about something, but it was pretty fucked up the one thing the Horsemen of the Apocalypse could agree on was that *Spaceballs* was an excellent movie.

FIVE

Did *Spaceballs* ever get old? Because Miss Mabel showed me this movie during movie night at her apartment, and it was still funny. Now that I thought about it, all the angels and Nephilim I'd met so far seemed to dig Mel Brooks. Miss Mabel exposed me to his entire cinematography, and I couldn't see why anyone *wouldn't* love the man, but was there something I didn't know?

"Fess up. What's the deal with Mel Brooks? Miss Mabel loved him too. Is he some sort of angel?"

Dice just laughed.

"No, he's just super clever. I think everyone loves Mel Brooks, Speedy, not just the Heavenly creatures."

"Yeah, but the three of you never agree about *anything.*"

Leif finally seemed to have forgotten about the gum on the door and was back to himself. His serene smile was back now that I was snuggled in between him and Aeron.

"There's plenty we agree on. You just haven't been around us long enough. When it used to be an option, we could even agree on where we wanted to go to eat every night."

I scoffed.

"You're all so different, and you like different things. You expect me to believe you're that old and you successfully maneuvered going out to eat?"

Dice just slung his leg over the arm of his chair and chewed on this toothpick.

"I think you forget how old we are. Sometimes, our options were shit and utter shit. Gruel used to be the only thing available. Gruel and ale so watered down, you might as well not bother. There wasn't always a Maria there that could whip up amazing gruel either. Leif is spoiled."

Leif didn't snap. He just kissed the top of my head and smiled at Dice.

"You cleaned your plate and had seconds."

"We have a fire pit, a vegetable plot, and farm animals in Florida. We also fish and hunt game. Still, no one in Florida has Maria's gifts in the kitchen. Sorry, Ariel, we have food, but it's not delicious Mexican food."

I just shrugged.

"I'm still remembering my past, but I don't think I'm a picky eater. As long as my belly is full, I'm happy."

Dice just smirked.

"That's because you've never had gruel. Our food isn't bad, and it's pretty fucking amazing when we get to have a base-wide barbeque because the hunters lucked out, or we have to put an animal down. It's just not Maria. Do you think she would come to Florida with us?"

"Dice," Leif warned. "Maria is not my personal chef. I'm hoping when we leave, she runs for a bigger political office than she had before and helps with the rebuilding. Just because she happens to be cooking for me now doesn't mean you can take her to Florida to cook for your grunts."

"She can be Governor to the grunts! God knows we'll need someone running a militarized state when this is over."

"So, do what people did before World War III and dictators. Hold an election. We're going to have to elect an entirely new government when we get rid of Isaiah."

Dice popped his toothpick in his mouth.

"That's Asher's territory. I just blow shit up."

That sounded pretty fucking ominous, and that was when it hit me. When we got to Florida, we were going to be letting the Horseman of War experiment on nuclear weapons.

I did not survive all this just to get blow up right before curtain call because Dice cut the wrong wire.

Six

I hardly knew Dice, and I had my reservations about being in the entire state of Florida while he was playing with explosives. Still, it just felt fucking awkward to make him sleep on the couch. It would probably feel weird to have him in bed too, but we were all snuggled into bed while Dice snored on the couch. And the Horseman of War could snore.

He also apparently rose with the sun. I didn't sleep in this time. I woke up when Leif and Aeron did. Dice was already awake and had sent for food. He still didn't have a shirt on. He had suspenders on again, and this time, they were *Sesame Street.* It was weird seeing a hulking angel with a red mohawk wearing suspenders with Oscar the Grouch all over them, but I would say this for Dice—he fucking *owned* those Oscar the Grouch suspenders.

As soon as we sat down to eat, he shoved a piece of paper at Leif and another at Aeron.

"See if you can get me everything on that list. How much serum will the device contain? I need to plan."

"Fifty gallons should be enough for several states if you can rig the bomb correctly."

"Exactly how many bombs do you have anyway, Dice?" I asked.

Weren't bombs super scarce? Not even my father had bombs anymore, or he'd used them. How did Dice even have spare bombs lying around? Why was I having this conversation?

"Oh, did they not tell you the real reason the war ended? It's not because Isaiah and his dictator friends got together and declared peace. That's just what they want people to think."

"Does it have anything to do with the toy bombs you have lying around Florida?"

Dice threw back his head and laughed.

"Honey, I've got spare bombs all over the world. I went around recruiting entire battalions and squads. I caused a damned mutiny in every area of the military until I had armies all over the world. I set a chain of command, then set up communication. It was beautiful. At the same time, all across the world, we organized a raid and stole all their bombs. I even got the ones the government wants to keep secret. They *had* to end the war because they didn't have a single bomb left, and all their soldiers were slowly joining me. They didn't have anyone left to kill for them."

Remember when people used to collect sane things like Pokémon? Pepperidge Farm remembers.

"Thank you for keeping that brief," Aeron said. "He likes to tell that story when he's drunk, but it's usually a lot more flowery and long-winded."

"Hey, I ended World War III and stole all the bombs. I think I've earned some bragging rights."

"Leif made serums to end this, and he doesn't have a fat head."

"Hey, you *all* deserve bragging rights. How many times have you defeated the Antichrist now? None of us would be here right now if it weren't for all of you. I'll tell Asher the same when I meet him," I said.

Everyone just started laughing. And I got the feeling they were laughing *at* me too. Dice slung his leg over the arm of the chair again and started swinging his knee.

"The Horseman of Conquest is scared shitless of that painting you did and probably won't allow himself to be alone in the same room with you. He wants Aeron to drop you off in California before you even come to Florida because he doesn't want me to get attached too. It's the whole three against one thing."

I felt my eyebrows rise to my hairline. What the fuck? Was Asher scared of me? If he was the same size as Aeron, Leif, and Asher, then he was probably massive. I looked tiny next to them.

"The Horseman of Conquest is scared of a girl?" I scoffed.

"No, he's scared of intimacy," Leif said. "He's close with us, but he never lets anyone else in. He'll have to get over it. We'll take you back to California if you want to go, but I'd prefer to have you with us."

I didn't even have to think about it. The smarter thing would be to go back to Miss Mabel and wait this out. I just couldn't. I *needed* to be in D.C. I could feel it in my bones. Something was going to happen. I wasn't feeling the urge to draw and grab my charcoal, but something was coming. I needed to be there with them, and it was more than just seeing my father die.

If there was any time for this Harbinger shit to kick in,

now was it. Why couldn't I get something I could control like the Horsemen? That would sure come in handy right now. It was like being constipated. It was precisely like eating peanut butter straight from the jar for dinner, then spending the next two days stopped up and miserable.

I ran my fingers through my hair.

"I need to be there. I just can't see why."

"Don't force it or that vein in your forehead will pop," Dice said.

See? Even Dice could see it was exactly like constipation. That nasty forehead vein showed up. I changed the subject.

"What are we doing today?"

"I'm coordinating with the other labs to get the serums up and running."

"I'm killing things."

"I'm therapizing your ass," Dice said.

"Why does that sound way kinkier than it needs to?" I said.

All Dice did was wink at me.

Seven

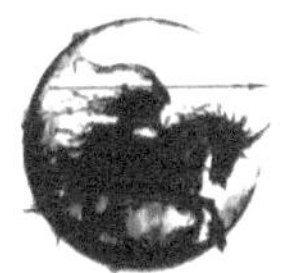

Aeron said he was going off to kill things again, but he was still hanging around, and he was getting possessive. Dice was still perched in his chair, and Aeron was to the point he was about to pee on my leg to claim me. Dice and I hadn't even gotten the chance to start talking because Aeron kept glowering at him.

"Aeron, what's your deal? Before Dice got here, you were acting like my painting was going to come true whether I wanted it to or not, and now you're about to start alpha male humping my leg."

"Dude, you're totally about to start humping her leg."

"Shut up, Dice!" Aeron barked.

I eased out from Aeron's arm so I could look him in the eye.

"Seriously, what's up?"

Aeron shrugged and deflated.

"I don't know! I thought we could all be one happy family until Dice showed up early. I'm fine with you and Leif, but for some reason, Dice showing up because of that painting really pisses me off."

I guess I was playing therapist today because Aeron and Dice needed to work through some shit. They both seemed convinced Dice was soon to be a part of this relationship, but there was just something about him that made me nervous. Probably because he had toy bombs and didn't seem to be afraid of anything.

"Okay, so this would be a therapy session. Let's be adults and talk about our feelings."

Dice started laughing.

"Aeron's favorite thing."

"Shut up, Dice!"

Is this what Leif meant about Dice and Aeron feeding off each other, and his shit got broken? If they got into a fistfight, I wouldn't be able to break it up. They'd trash this entire room before I could get Leif. Leif was back at the other lab, and I still didn't have a phone. If I could talk on the whole angel frequency they used to communicate on, no one had taught me how.

"Hey! No poking the Horseman of Death, Dice. Aeron, stop letting him get to you. I thought the two of you were friends?"

"We are," they both said.

I just threw up my hands.

"Then why aren't you acting like it?"

"Exactly!" Dice yelled. "You were the one talking her up to me when you dropped the bomb about the painting. If you'll recall, I wasn't all that wild to find out a Harbinger painted me kissing her."

He wasn't? Well, that was just offensive. I wasn't wild to have found myself painting an orgy with strangers when I saw it, and I still didn't want to do it, but what kind of guy found out someone who could paint the future painted you banging and got mad about it? Wait, there were two of them. The Horseman of War and the Horseman of Conquest didn't want any part of the White House orgy. Which, yeah, I was a little butt hurt they didn't want to fuck me, but relieved at the same time because I still didn't think I'd be in a fucking mood after I saw my father again. Even if I did come to care for them like I did Leif and Aeron, I couldn't see confronting my father again and one of us killing him, and it leading to that.

Could I see myself getting drunk on moonshine and passing out? Totally.

Aeron let out this irritated grunt.

"I know it doesn't make sense, and I know I tried to talk both of you into this. I swear I was okay with it until Dice appeared and started trying to get Speedy alone."

I started playing with Aeron's hair.

"But *why* does it bother you? You walked in on Leif and me and we've all been together that way. Dice and I hardly know each other. We just talked when he got me alone. I hardly know Dice, and I don't know Asher at all. Asher seems against the entire thing. Dice may get to know me and think I'm annoying."

They both just started shaking their heads at me like I had no idea what I was talking about, and they knew better. I *loathed* when people looked at me like that, even if it was a topic I was totally unqualified to argue against. Just because you knew something someone else might not didn't mean you had to be a snob about it.

And I was right about this. That painting was totally in my control. We stopped fucking Nazis because of something I drew. None of them would press me if I said no to a fucking free for all next to my father's corpse. I didn't think any of them would ask for sex either, even with that painting out in the world now. I wished I had destroyed that thing instead of hanging it over my bed. I wished I could remember why I hung it in pride of place instead of burning it.

"You're a Harbinger, Ariel. Things are going to be set in motion that by the time we get to the White House, we're all going to be together. The painting may not progress past you kissing all of us, and it might never have been an orgy. But we will all make it to the White House and we will all at least kiss you," Dice said.

"Unless I say no. I don't care what I am, what I painted, or what's going on in the world. I still have the right to say no."

Aeron pulled me to his chest and kissed the top of my head.

"She's going to say no just to prove a point, no matter how she feels when we get there."

"Yeah, I get that vibe."

"I'm sorry. I was raised human and it's weird to be told you're going to develop feelings for people you don't know just because of a painting you did. All of you might accept it, but it's fucking bizarre."

"With the shit you read?" Aeron scoffed. "You know I read *Blood Feud* too, right? Do you remember that? Your vampire mistress has five fated mates she learned about when she kills a witch. She thinks the witch is full of shit until she's about to drain the blood from someone else and tastes their blood for the first time. You raved about that entire series and you think it's weird your painting is going to come true?"

I threw up my hands and shrieked. I was trying really hard not to punch Aeron.

"That was fiction! It was about a vampire coven of

assassins that killed and fucked things. Shifters have fated mates too, but we aren't going around sniffing and biting each other and you don't have magic dicks that grow when you fuck."

Dice was looking at me like I had a second head.

"What kind of shit are you reading, Speedy? I can't even find shit like that on porn sites."

"You're looking at the wrong porn then," I snapped.

Dice perked right up.

"Go on."

Aeron just rolled his eyes.

"Porn doesn't exist anymore. Read *Blood Feud*. Leif has a copy and it's pretty graphically illustrated and I think all of us she got to read it enjoyed it."

Dice just stretched.

"I can't believe we've regressed to illustrated porn."

"It's *not* porn. It has a plot."

"I think *you're* looking at the wrong porn, Speedy. All the good porn has a plot."

"*Blood Feud* is not porn! I'll bet you're going to tell me you think romance novels are lady porn because you're a misogynist fuck."

Aeron and Dice were laughing at me. Dice leaned his elbows on his knees and winked at me.

"I went through my *Team Jacob* period. Edward is just a creepy, controlling man child."

I started choking on my water. Aeron pounded me on the back.

"The fucking Horseman of War read *Twilight?*"

Aeron groaned.

"He requested special trips to Earth to watch the movies. Dice loves his lady porn."

"Some of us are in touch with our romantic sides and don't quote Bruce Willis to get laid."

Aeron wrapped his enormous arm around my shoulder.

"Bruce hasn't failed me yet."

Were they getting along now? The tension in Aeron's body had left and he wasn't glowering at Leif anymore. You couldn't cut the air in the room with a knife right now. That's what I loved about *Blood Feud*. Polyamorous vampire assassins just had the power to bring people together. It could even calm a grumpy, jealous angel. Wait a minute.

"Doesn't Heaven look down on you watching porn?"

"Only humans are so interested in what goes on in other people's bedrooms, Ariel," Dice said. "Rape is a crime and a sin, but there's not some peeping angel out there making a list of all the kinky shit you do behind closed doors to throw it in your face as a reason not to let you in. As long as everything is consensual, Heaven isn't really into kink shaming, despite what humans would have everyone think."

"That's so different than everything I've ever thought. I never thought I'd meet angels, but I wouldn't have expected them to be anything like the three of you."

Dice and Aeron were both beaming at me like telling them they weren't like how they had been portrayed to all of humanity was a compliment. I mean, they swore, Aeron and I stole, and I'd had sex with Leif and Aeron. That didn't fit any image of angels I'd ever read about in my entire life. I certainly pictured them in long flowing white robes and not crazy suspenders.

"Some of the angels who never leave Heaven have that whole insufferably pure thing going on and they look down on us that enjoy Earthly pleasures. As far as they are concerned, they never want to come here and Heaven's version of the arts is by far superior."

"You mean it's not?"

Dice and Aeron were totally not fighting anymore. Now, I was seeing what Leif meant about them feeding off each other because they were acting like the best of friends now bad mouthing the other angels.

"Would you want to experience music, books, and cinema written by angels who have never experienced a hard day in their entire life? They haven't even had to deal with shitty weather. It's like having a fourteen-year-old sheltered child who lives a blessed life and has never even seen the news trying to write real world conflict," Aeron said. "It's more like watching *Teletubbies* and less like *Die Hard.*"

I felt my entire soul retreat up my asshole and my body involuntarily shuddered.

"Don't even mention *Teletubbies.* I fell asleep in front of the TV and woke up to that on. It was pretty much the most horrifying thing I've ever seen in my entire life. I've bashed the heads in on zombie corpses and those Teletubbies are still scarier."

"Okay, Speedy. Fess up. Truth or Dare. Who is scarier? Isaiah or that talking baby sun?" Dice said.

"What if I wanted to pick dare?"

"Then I dare you to answer that question."

"You're going to get me in so much trouble, aren't you?"

"Only if you let me. Now, inquiring minds want to know. Who is scarier? The Antichrist or the Teletubbies?"

I don't think I'd ever been asked a more fucked up or loaded question in my entire life and I'd had plenty of fucked up conversations while high with Miss Mabel and my softball team. It was kind of like the time someone on my softball team asked who would win in a fight between King Kong and Jaws. There's basically no place for that fight to take place without giving one the advantage except for outer space.

"That's kind of a loaded question."

"I'm curious too," Aeron said.

"It'll help us protect you when we get to D.C. We still don't know how you're going to react. We have no way of knowing until we get there."

"Well, Teletubbies aren't real. My father is. Look what he's managed to accomplish so far. Teletubbies freak me out, but I'm definitely much more afraid of him since he's flesh."

"No one is judging for being afraid of seeing him again," Aeron said. "Just keep in mind you'll have four angels as backup."

Dice popped his toothpick out his mouth and started swinging his leg again.

"*Personally,* I think that talking sun baby is way more terrifying than the son of Satan and I don't care who judges me."

"Now that we've gotten the Teletubby talk out of the way and Dice has officially proclaimed he's *Team Jacob,* are the two of you good now?"

"I was never bad," Dice said. "Aeron was the one humping your leg in a show of dominance."

"There may be some residual leg humping, but I'm feeling much better about Dice jumping the gun and coming here. I still think he should be playing with his bombs, but you need to learn to use your grace as a weapon, and Dice would be best at teaching that."

Dice just couldn't let it sit. We were finally making progress, and he had to shoot his mouth off.

"Good. Now get the fuck out and go kill things. She's not going to learn a damned thing with you manhandling her."

Aeron just stood up and flung his hair out his eyes.

"She *likes* the way I manhandle her. She clawed my back up when I manhandled her in the shower."

"You're leg humping again," I pointed out.

"Oh, fine," Aeron said, stomping out.

Dice wasn't even phased. When I turned back to him, he was chewing on his toothpick again.

"I'm shocked that it didn't take longer. Back to you, Speedy."

My heart started racing. I much preferred when Dice's attention was on Aeron and not me.

EIGHT

Dice's idea of dealing with my feelings before I faced my father seemed to have no rhyme or reason. After Aeron left, he was hyper-focused on talking about Teletubbies and my feelings about the one time I saw the show. What that had to do with my father, I had no idea. I didn't think Dice did either. I think the reason he made me so nervous was that he was completely random and unpredictable.

It seemed like he was going somewhere with the whole Teletubby thing, then he just dropped it. It was driving me a little mad.

"So, tell me about your first love."

I narrowed my eyes at him. What the fuckity fuck did that have to do with any of this?

"I'm sorry, but what does that have to do with Isaiah or Teletubbies for that matter? You know a lot of my past is missing, right?"

"But you remembered the Teletubbies."

"Don't ever mention Teletubbies again, or I swear, I'll get Aeron to teach me this."

I was so deadly serious about that that if the next words out of his mouth involved that show, I was getting up and walking out. Where was he even going with this? Dice just held up his hands like I was going to punch him in the face.

"Just hear me out, Ariel. You seem to get your memories back when people say certain things. You remember you saw that show, and it freaked you out. It's a seemingly insignificant memory in the grand scheme of things, but you got it back. There might be some memory lost in your lizard brain that could help you beat him. Think about it. Why else would he have summoned Satan to take them? Isaiah isn't stupid. He must have known it only would have been a matter of time before we found you. I'm sure he intended to get some sort of intel and moving you, but he would have known eventually, we would have found you.

"We have all his research. We know most of his crimes. There isn't much about him that we *don't* know except things that might have been said behind closed doors in front of a child. He could have asked you to do something or done something to you that helps us get close to him. Getting your memories back is important."

"Aren't I going to go insane if I remember all at once?"

"If you try to force it. We're just having a conversation and seeing if it jogs anything loose."

"About Teletubbies!"

"I believe it was you that said not to bring that up again. I just kept you talking about it to see if you could remember anything else about that day?"

"So, there was some sort of method to your Teletubby madness?"

Dice just smirked at me.

"I *always* have a plan. It just takes other people time to recognize my genius."

"Like stealing every single remaining bomb in the world and making a bomb toy chest?"

"I do love my explosives, but the alternative was waiting until they ran out and that involved dropping them on innocent people, and your father was going to make damned sure the war didn't end until it absolutely had to."

"True."

"And we needed them because Leif was planning mass delivery with aerosol. I just need to neuter the total mass destruction aspect."

"It's a bomb, not a golden retriever!"

"You're so focused on my bombs when you need to be worrying about remembering."

"I'm sorry, I didn't realize there was a cure-all for Satan induced memory loss, and everyone has been telling me remembering too much is dangerous."

"That's why we're just having a chat. Now, first love. Go."

"I don't think I've ever allowed myself to get attached that way until I met Leif and Aeron. You might not have noticed, but kids tend to have trust issues when their father is the Antichrist and experiments on them."

"Then Aeron and Leif are lucky angels. Fair enough. What's your earliest happy memory?"

"I already know that. I remembered it with Leif. It was my first Christmas with Miss Mabel."

"Do you remember Christmas with Isaiah?"

"He didn't celebrate holidays. He'd throw big parties for his birthday, but it was always to network with senators and people in business. They never allowed me to attend, but sometimes, I would sneak out and watch. He would always pitch a fit if there were a politician he wanted in his pocket, and they declined his invitation."

"He was only able to get that supplement in the water because of his government connections."

I had a flash of one of his parties and got excited because it didn't seem to make any sense.

"He also wanted clergy at his parties. He never talked to me about the importance of believing, but the only time he ever went to church was when he wanted another pastor or bishop in his back pocket. He pretended to be so many different religions. He'd be Catholic one week, and Baptist the next. There was this Rabbi he wanted. He called Isaiah a *gonif* and banned him from his synagogue. Isaiah pitched this huge fit about that.

"He threw me in my padded room and demanded I draw something big. He left me in there for a week because he didn't like what I was drawing. He eventually let me out because he was excited about this pastor that just got elected to Congress, but I never found out what the big deal about that particular conquest was."

"I can tell you."

Right then, my vision started getting hazy, and my hand felt itchy. This was *not* the time for my Harbinger side to come out and play. I had a feeling that particular politician was important because it excited my father when he got elected. He left me alone for an entire month because he was making phone calls trying to get an introduction.

I tried to suppress it. I'd never done that before. Could it just wait ten minutes so I could find out how that man played into my father's whole diabolical plan? I didn't ask for charcoal. I sat there, trying to listen to Dice. It wasn't working. The more I tried to suppress it and not draw, the more the ringing in my ears drowned out Dice.

Dice knew something was wrong. He jumped up and started shaking me, but it was like I was paralyzed. He touched my face, and I could see blood on his fingers through the haze of black in my vision. It was like my entire body seized up in a cramp. I couldn't have even held a piece of charcoal if I was able to ask for it.

I felt my body seizing as my vision narrowed to a tiny point. The ringing in my ears was practically a roar. I couldn't hold on anymore. I blacked out.

NINE

My eyes fluttered open. I was flat on my back on the bed with the Horsemen of the Apocalypse flittering over me. My head could only be in Dice's lap because I could see Aeron. Leif was right in my face, and was that his finger in my ear? It felt weird, and I tried to shove it out.

"Get your fucking finger out my ear, Leif," I moaned.

I felt like a flaming garbage truck had hit me. My head was pounding, my muscles were sore, and it tasted like something crawled in my mouth and died.

"I'm just taking your temperature. See? It's normal. What exactly happened, Ariel?"

I tried to remember. I'd never done this before when I didn't draw it out. I tried to recall what I'd seen when I blacked out. I tried to sit up, and they all pressed me back into Dice's lap. No, this was important. We needed to be ready.

"Stop! I was trying to push down a vision to find out what Dice was going to tell me about one of my father's politicians, but I had a vision about him."

My head was spinning. This man was still alive, and he was utterly insane. Aeron handed me a thermos of water.

"Drink this before you tell us. And tell us lying down."

"I have to sit up to drink."

"Fine, but lie back down," Leif said, gently helping me sit up.

The water was cool and refreshing. It was as if pushing down that vision had depleted all the water in my body. I gulped the water down and collapsed back into Dice's lap. I hadn't even processed I was snuggling in his lap. It felt like it was the playoffs, and I'd played at least three softball games that day.

"You can't push it down when you get a vision, Ariel," Leif fussed.

"Calm down, Sparky. Who is the man Dice was telling me about? He was in my vision. He's alive, and I think he's on his way to Florida."

"What did you see?" Dice demanded.

"He was driving some RV he rigged up with fences and barbed wire. He's got this massive speaker on the top, and he's driving from D.C. screaming sermons through the speaker about repenting. He's got an entire horde following him. He's not quite there yet. I saw a road sign about New Jersey in my vision."

"I told you that you should have let me kill that fuck," Aeron growled.

"*Who* is that fuck? Dice triggered a memory. My father was very excited when he got elected."

Aeron just grumped at me.

"We aren't telling you a damned thing unless you lie back down and relax. You scared the shit out of us. We thought one of Leif's pets scratched you, and you were coming down with the Rage Mutation. Dice called us right away, and when we got here, you were totally limp and bleeding from the nose and ears. You can't ignore it when you feel a vision coming."

"Thank you, Captain Obvious. Lesson learned."

Dice just pulled me back into his lap and started playing with my hair. Okay, I'd never be mad at someone playing with my hair, even if I wasn't all that sure about Dice. Clearly, this man was somehow important, and he was continuing to cause problems if he was heading to Florida. People didn't take vacations anymore. Plus, no one stuck a speaker on an RV to scream *repent or go to Hell* for good reasons.

"Okay, fine. I'm settled. Who's the psycho?"

"Okay, remember how we told you the Book of Revelations had been altered to make the end of the world seem less dire? You would know Leonard Carmen as the Lion of Judah if you remember your scripture. In the bible, it's a heavenly persona who breaks the seven seals to signal the second coming of Christ. In layman's terms, it's really the Antichrist's errand person to bring about the end of the world," Aeron said.

"What a dick. Why didn't you just kill him before he managed to cause all this?"

"It doesn't work like that in this day and age. Leonard wasn't working alone. He was a preacher who got elected to Congress. He had other politicians, his constituents, his congregation, and lobbyist on his side. If he had disappeared without a trace or been assassinated, he would have been turned into a martyr to his people. They would have pressed harder to get his bills pushed through," Aeron said.

"Plus, it was hard to narrow it down to Leonard with

all the politicians talking about the exact same thing. He was meticulous," Leif said.

I just blinked. I was so confused. I got that he was a tool, but I didn't get why.

"Why would a preacher help the Antichrist?"

"Easy. Do you remember the year you went missing? What it was like in the world? People were so convinced there were wars on Christmas, and social media was censoring religious posts. All Isaiah had to do was swoop in and prey on those fears. He just had to lie about the devil people feared while hiding his true face. They were all too willing to be his pawn if it meant fighting a false religious war," Leif said.

Well, there was my why. People could be nuts about that kind of thing. Miss Mabel was continually ranting about her social media friends from her bridge club being idiots posting that kind of stuff.

"Well, what do we do? He's on his way to Florida."

All three angels just beamed at me.

"Not yet," Dice said. "We checked in with Asher and sent our horses. He's still outfitting his RV. He won't leave for another few weeks or so."

"Why doesn't one of your murder horses just kill him before he leaves?"

Dice grinned at me, and that was when I realized he was utterly insane.

"Well, he's bringing Rage Heads, right? They'll all be in one place to kill. Think about it. He'll be dragging Rage Heads all the way from D.C. We can wipe out a good bit of them by letting him get a little close. Let the little whippersnapper think he's accomplishing something and cross several states. We'll kill him in Georgia."

"Okay, but wouldn't it be best just to kill him now?" I asked.

"Maybe, but it would be way less fun."

Dice was going to get me in so much trouble.

TEN

No one seemed as nervous as me that a nutbag preacher was on his way to Florida dragging zombies, but then again, I didn't have murder horses to check other states like they did. Aeron and Leif seemed on board with Dice's plan to let Leonard get a bunch of zombies in one place and drop a bomb on them. Was it just me, or was that fucked up? Why not just have Asher kill him before he left? I was getting way too comfortable with murder.

It was also pretty fucked up talking to Dice like a therapist. His topics were super random, but what was even more fucked up was that I was remembering. I hadn't hit some golden nugget that would help us beat Isaiah, but I was getting more of my past back.

It wasn't much. It was childhood memories and things after I ran, but I held onto it. As far as I was concerned, the more I got back, the better. It was like a part of me was missing because there was so much I couldn't remember. My father made it a point to take that from me, but what was lurking in my memories that he wanted to hide?

Dice and I were in our usual positions. I was on one end of the couch, and he was one the other. I had a bowl of salsa in my lap, and he had a bowl of guac on his chest. Dice could mow through so much guacamole, it shocked me Mexico wasn't having an avocado shortage. Or, for that matter, why I hadn't caused a tomato shortage yet with my salsa consumption.

Dice's feet were on me like they usually were, but for some reason, it didn't bother me. Not like it did knowing he was sleeping on the couch while I slept with Aeron and Leif, but that was a conversation I could have with my lizard brain much later.

"There's an important memory we haven't touched on yet."

"What's that?"

"The day you got kidnapped."

I stopped with a chip halfway to my mouth. A big blob of salsa dropped right on my boob. I ignored the way Dice's eyes fell to it, and he licked his lips.

"Do we have to talk about that?"

"Yes, but not until you are ready. Something might have happened when you got to that lab that could help you beat him. I don't think you were awake when Satan visited, but I doubt they kept you sedated the entire ride to Washington State. Something might have been said. Isaiah could have said something when he saw you again. You know the kind of movies Aeron likes to watch. The madman always reveals their plans when they think they've gained the upper hand."

I made a farting noise with my mouth and scooped

the salsa off my boob with my finger. I licked it off and pointed at Dice.

"You're right, but way to traumatize a girl. How exactly am I supposed to remember that?"

"By not forcing it. You remember Aeron. Think about how excited you were to meet him for the first time."

"Leif too."

"Stop stalling."

"Quit rushing me."

"Focus on Aeron and Leif. You had been talking to them online for months. You had painted all of us together, and you were excited to meet them. You remember doing the painting. Try to remember the days after that."

It was like Dice's smooth voice hypnotized me. I found myself slipping into the past. I was years younger, and my hair was much pinker then. Aeron and Leif. I was excited to meet them. What the fuck happened then? I knew we were supposed to meet at my favorite falafel place. Why didn't I tell him to pick me up at home? I felt like I was falling into a trance.

I want to leave right away. Aeron and I are supposed to have a quick dinner and then hit the road. I know if I ask him to pick me up at my apartment, we are going to sit and chat, so I ask him to meet me at the restaurant. My heart is pounding in my ears. My bag is packed, but I change clothes four times. Miss Mabel knows I'm leaving, and she's going to watch my apartment. We have plans to come back here after we beat my father and start some hippie love community with the three of us.

I don't take my car. The restaurant is within walking distance. I lace up my rollerblades and skate to the restau-

rant. Aeron is already there. I can see him in the window. I'm still across the street. I'm waiting for the light to change, then I'll skate across the street to meet him.

I'm waiting at the stoplight when a van pulls up to the curb. It's almost too fast to notice. Three men jump out the back of the van and grab me. They weren't counting on me being on rollerblades, and we all nearly face plant on the pavement. I fight as hard as I can, but they have something over my mouth, and I can't scream.

It must be chloroform because the harder I try to breathe and scream, the hazier everything gets. I blackout just as they throw me in the back of the van. I never even had a chance to cry for help, and it happened so fast, no one even saw me get abducted.

I gasped as I came out of my memory. Aeron needed to be here. Aeron blamed my entire abduction on himself, but those men were organized and had their faces covered. It might not have had anything to do with him.

"Get Aeron!"

I'd hardly gotten the sentence out when Aeron practically kicked the door in. I was pretty grateful for the whole angel radio thing, but what exactly did Dice tell him? Aeron looked like he was ready to kill anything in the room that wasn't us, and his sword was out. His chest was heaving, and his eyes darted around the room.

"What is it?" he demanded.

"I remember the day they took me. I'm not in danger."

Aeron's sword disappeared, and his eyes cut to Dice.

"You seriously need to work on your communication skills. When you pop into my head and tell me Ariel needs me and she's supposed to be safe with you, I expect the worst!"

"You're such an alpha male, Aeron," Dice groaned. "Ariel can still need you without you having to kill something. Boyfriends talk about feelings too, you twat. You can't kill those."

"Let's just chalk this up to miscommunication," I said before they started fighting again. "Aeron, I remembered the day I was taken. It was coordinated and planned. It happened right across the street from the restaurant in broad daylight. It was so fast, and I don't think anyone saw it. I know that intersection. A lot of drug deals go down there because there are no cameras on the street. I should have either picked a different place to eat or just had you pick me up at my apartment, so we could immediately disappear. I thought if you picked me up there, we'd never leave because we'd get stuck chatting or furiously making out."

Aeron ran his fingers through his hair and started pacing.

"I should have known. I should have insisted on picking you up. I should have bought you a plane ticket and never crossed the border!"

"Man, you're both going to drive yourselves insane with all the what-ifs. Neither of you could have known because we didn't get into his secret server until a year after I was called. You could only see what he didn't mind other people seeing."

"I should have gotten better at hacking," Aeron grumbled.

I walked over and wrapped my arms around his waist. I buried my face in his chest and nuzzled him with my cheek. I was about to say something, but Dice beat me to it.

"You are good at hacking. I taught all of you. We

haven't been called in a while, remember? We had to get used to modern technology before I could get into Isaiah's things. It took me a year, and I'm the best, remember?"

"It's no one's fault but Isaiah's," I said.

"The Nephilim speaks the truth."

Aeron cupped my chin and lifted my face to his.

"You're making progress with your memories. That's good because Leif will be ready to go to Florida in three days. He's going to be holding a mass vaccination party, and then we are leaving."

"To take care of that crazy preacher?"

Dice and Aeron just laughed.

"He's still trying to stockpile enough gas in his RV to make it to Florida. Remember when I said most people don't use cars anymore?" Aeron said.

"The Nazis had trucks."

Aeron just grunted.

"It made it easier to make them go all explody."

"It's a stupid plan, Ariel," Dice said. "Think about it. He's trying to drag zombies from several states into Florida, but the logistics are flawed. He's going to have to stop and refuel several times. He can strip the RV to make room for fuel, but what about supplies and a place to sleep? He can't drive that long without stopping to sleep, even if you take refueling out the equation. How is he going to start driving again when he's surrounded by Rage Heads? They tend to clog up engines when you plow through them."

"Ew."

Aeron just shrugged.

"We know he gets to New Jersey because you saw the sign. The chances of him making it to Florida without getting eaten are slim to nothing."

"I still don't understand why we aren't killing him. My father couldn't have done all this without him."

Dice just shook his head.

"It's not possible to kill everyone who helped your father just yet. He had his fingers in a lot of plots. We need to focus on the big picture, not all the minor players. We need to kill the Rage Heads, get that vaccine to everyone, and kill Isaiah. Once that's done, we have to rebuild the entire world. There will be trials, and people will get their justice."

Aeron pulled me into a hug.

"You'll get your revenge, Speedy, but other people need it too. Every single person alive right now has lost someone. They either got killed in the war, or they had to watch a loved one turn into a Rage Head. Somewhere out there, someone is wondering if a friend or a family member that went out to scout for supplies and never came home is wandering around as a Rage Head, dead, or they had to hole up somewhere because their path home was blocked. They'll never get those answers. We can only make sure the people responsible pay in the public eye so they can get closure."

I squared my shoulders. I thought I was coming to Mexico because they needed my blood. Leif did what he needed to, and we made progress. But I wasn't done yet.

They took my memories for a reason. I had to get them back.

ELEVEN

Dice was excellent about coaxing random memories out, but aside from the day they abducted me, I still hadn't remembered anything significant. I suppose I should be grateful for getting little things back. I was feeling a little more whole, but the entire reason they took my memories wasn't becoming clear. It wasn't like I could force it either.

I was starting to like my chats with Dice. He was easy to talk to, even if he never wore a shirt. He seemed to have this wide array of bizarre suspenders. I think my favorite so far was the Baby Yoda ones. He certainly wore them well.

Aeron wanted to spend more time with Dice and I. I knew part of it was boredom, but most of it was him knowing I might remember something traumatic and wanting to be there for me. It was nice, but sometimes, he interrupted Dice when he was on a roll.

I didn't see much of Leif, and I missed him. He was working hard at the lab, and I only ever saw him at night and breakfast. We weren't exactly getting our sexing on with Dice on the couch. It was feeling more and more wrong to have Dice on the sofa, but I was trying to ignore that emotion.

After a few days of feeling like a total failure because I hadn't figured out why my memories had been taken, we ran out of time. Dice couldn't help me because he was organizing the military to set up the massive amounts of vaccines that would be going out.

They were setting up checkpoints all over the state and taking people from California. Aeron worked it out with Jade that the gangs and military in Mexico would safely exchange the vaccines at the border. There were still doctors in California that could give people the vaccinations.

I was going to help out as much as I could. I was pretty handy with a needle when it came to tattooing people, but you pretty much wouldn't want to trust me to draw blood or deliver a vaccine. I was just going to stand around threatening people with Smurfette, which is where I was needed.

It was time. We met an entire squad of soldiers and loaded up into a black SUV. See? People still used cars instead of murder horses. We drove to the gate where there was a large military presence and tents set up. There was already a line inside the wall and snaking around the booby traps outside.

Men and women with guns escorted us to the tent. I was pretty shocked when Aeron and Dice took a seat and started vaccinating people. I felt pretty left out. I was the only person in our group *not* giving people shots. I was just standing there, awkwardly with my baby blue bat.

People were emotional. They were weeping and thanking everyone as they got their vaccines. It was beautiful. Everyone was coming together to make sure people lived through this.

Most people knew it was Leif that came up with the vaccine, and he had a little fan club. Everyone seemed shocked he was out there vaccinated people himself. He had an entire table to himself, and it was slowly filling with gifts. The area behind him was starting to get pretty full too. Everyone just wanted to thank him. I noticed they had gifts for everyone. Even if Leif didn't give them their shot, they gave a small token to the person that did before they brought something over to Leif.

We were out there all day and all night, and it was pretty drama free until we started to get to the end of the line. I saw dust kicking up as some vehicles approached. Men began spilling out of trucks. They had blue bandanas covering their faces, and they started shoving people towards the end of the line and trying to cut.

"I think that's my cue," I said, swinging Smurfette over my shoulder and walking towards them.

Dice and Aeron flanked me on either side.

"Did you think we would let you smash heads without us?" Aeron said.

"It feels like I haven't beaten someone up in ages," Dice sighed.

Five men were pushing their way through the line. I could see knives and guns strapped to their waists, but they hadn't drawn them yet.

"Is there a problem, boys?" I asked.

One of the men who must have been the leader started speaking in rapid-fire Spanish to another man, who stepped forward to address me.

"The pretty girl needs to step aside. We don't want to hurt you."

"Well, you see now, I don't want to hurt *you*. There's a line, and you're cutting. We aren't leaving until everyone has had their vaccination. If you go back to the end of the line, we won't have a problem."

Dice stepped forward and cracked his knuckles.

"But I wouldn't mind hurting you,"

Aeron drew his sword from behind his back.

"Me either. Are we going to have a problem here?"

Two of the men reached for their guns. Dice's sword was out in an instance. Aeron and Dice made slashing motions, and both men's holsters fell to the ground. The other men started shouting and drew their weapons. We had three guns trained on us.

"Go ahead. Make my day," Aeron said.

I groaned. This was *not* the time for movie quotes. Dice darted between them and addressed the man that spoke English.

"Tell your friends we can make all of them dead before they can fire a shot. Just go to the back of the line!"

He tried screaming over his friends, but they were all shouting in Spanish and waving guns in our faces. They finally decided to listen.

"You can get vaccinated, or you can get dead," Dice warned.

The man relayed his message, and that seemed to get through to them. They put their guns away and grumbled as they went to the back of the line. They were one of the few groups that brought drama instead of gifts, but they got their vaccinations.

The sun was coming up by the time we got home, but everyone who came got vaccinated. Leif had been talking into an earpiece the entire time. When we finally fell into bed, he nuzzled my neck.

"It was a success. All my contacts said we vaccinated everyone who came, and California got the vaccines they needed. We gave them enough to share, and we have an understanding with Jade to spread the word and hand them off to people at the gate who ask for them."

"Excellent. I'm exhausted," Aeron said.

I finally had to say it. We were going to leave for Florida soon. I had no idea what the sleeping arrangements were going to be there, but it seriously felt like we were excluding Dice, and we had the room.

"Dice, get your ass in here and sleep with us," I hollered.

I didn't have to ask him twice. He came bounding in and dove under the covers. Aeron didn't say a damned thing. He seemed pretty pleased I finally asked.

TWELVE

The angels beat me awake, but they usually did. They were going through Leif's loot and eating breakfast. I joined them on the couch and started eating. We would be leaving this place soon, and I was seriously going to miss it. San Quintin had become like a second home to me.

Leif handed me a pretty red necklace with red beads on it.

"She said it was for the pretty girl who helped me. This is for you."

"Someone made me a gift?" I asked, slipping it over my head.

"It's Santeria. It's called Ormosia Spp, and it's made from peony seeds. It's supposed to give protection."

I fingered the red seeds. I could use all the protection I could get. I wished I could find the woman who made this and thank her.

"I hope you thanked her for me."

Leif just beamed at me.

"I'd never insult her and not do that. We have a lot of protection charms along with food. Are you ready to leave, Ariel? We've done everything we can here. Dice and I are going to take you to his base in Florida, and Aeron is going to make a quick stop in Gabriel's Haven to drop off vaccines and let them know help is coming."

I threw my arms around Aeron's neck. I could just lovingly strangle him for helping Gabriel's Haven like that when we no longer needed to go back there.

"Have I told you how much I love you? Thank you for helping them."

Aeron held me at arm's length, and he looked grumpy again. What was it now? Was he ever in a good mood?

"Ariel, do you realize you just told me you loved me? Were you serious?"

Well, shit. Had I not said that before? And the first time I did, I did it like that? I was so bad at this. Most people tried to pick the perfect moment for this, and it just dropped out my mouth like I expected him to know it already. I grabbed Leif's hand.

"I love both of you. I'm sorry I haven't said it before now. And despite my protests, I'm growing rather fond of Suspender Man too."

"I have that effect on people," Dice said.

"You're more like angel fungus," Aeron said.

"Do they ever stop?" I asked Leif.

"No. It just escalates until my shit gets broken."

"I would like to point out we vaccinated every one, and nothing got broken this time," Dice said. "We didn't even have to kill that gang that showed up and tried to cut in line."

Aeron just yawned.

"I wouldn't have been mad about killing some gang members, but there's the whole repopulating the earth thing when this is over. Their miscreant sperm could sire children that bring about a new age. Every sperm is sacred."

"That's gross, Aeron," I groaned.

"Aeron has never been able to phrase things very tactfully, but he's not wrong. He even managed to squeeze in a movie quote to make his point," Leif groaned.

"I *like* Aeron's movie quotes. Sometimes, they bring back memories. Monty Python, right? Miss Mabel was fond of those movies."

"Okay, girlfriend test, did *you* love the movies?" Aeron asked.

"What kind of person *doesn't* like Monty Python?" I asked.

"They exist, and you pretty much can't trust them," Aeron said.

"Ooh, look at this!" Leif squealed, pulling something out one of the boxes he got. "It's a hand-carved wooden cross. The detail is amazing!"

Dice just patted him on the shoulder.

"You know you can't take all this to Florida with you, right?"

Leif straight up stuck his tongue out at Dice like he wasn't a grown-ass angel.

"I know that, dipshit. I'm taking this cross, though."

"Leif loves it when they fangirl over him," Aeron said.

"Be nice. I fangirl over Leif all the time," I said. "I fangirl over all of you."

"Well, we need to get our shit together and get to Florida because I've got some bombs to play with."

That sobered up everyone in the room. Leif and Aeron went into full angel mode, and I just got terrified because I didn't even want to be in the same country as Dice and bombs.

Thirteen

There wasn't much to pack. Everything I owned right now could fit into a rucksack. I didn't even bother unpacking when we got to San Quintin. I thought developing a vaccine was going to take some time. Actually, way longer than it really did, but I knew we'd be moving again once it was done.

Leif packed his bag, and Aeron loaded up his rucksack. Dice came with no bags. He seemed to do that angel pockets thing to reach into his room back in Florida to grab new suspenders. I still didn't think it was fair I didn't get the angel pockets. Getting a nosebleed because I ignored a vision was just shitty.

Maria came in to say goodbye. She gave Leif a colossal hug and ruffled his hair.

"You're disappearing, aren't you?"

"I have to. We're going to end this, Maria."

"Will I see you again?"

"If you do, it will be because the Rage Heads are dead. Please spread the word. If you hear from us to stay inside, people need to keep inside their houses. It means we've found a delivery device to kill the Rage Heads. We're going to try to do it so it drops in unpopulated areas, but we have less of a chance of civilian casualties if no one is out."

Maria pulled Leif down and kissed his forehead.

"I'll spread the word. I'll miss you, Leif. I'm guessing when I walk out the door, all of you are going to mysteriously disappear the same way you came."

"We've done what we came here to do."

"I know. Peace be with you. All of you."

Maria disappeared, and I went to wrap my arms around Leif's waist.

"I'm going to miss her. If I could pick my mother, it would be her. We should go."

Did I mention I hated it when they disappeared me places without warning me? In the time it took me to blink, I was no longer standing in Leif's apartments in Mexico. I was in some sort of apartment that looked like a new age yoga studio. I was guessing this was Dice's apartment.

"Why does an angel have a statue of the Buddha?" I asked.

Dice flopped on a Papasan chair and winked at me.

"He was a wise man. My space, my rules. I'm *not* taking the couch here, and I get to snuggle with Ariel at least two nights a week."

"The fuck you are," Aeron growled.

Leif just laughed.

"We're going to have to deal with it, Aeron," Leif said. "Florida is Dice's territory. His word is the law here. We'll have to swap nights because I'm not giving up two nights snuggling because you're a grumpy fuck."

"Well, that's settled," Dice said, clapping his hands. He didn't even give Aeron a chance to argue. "Who wants a tour?"

I actually did want one. I'd never been to Florida before. My father never took me, and after I ran, Florida seemed way too close to New York to risk a trip. Plus, I had beaches in California, and we had Disneyland. I had no reason to make a trip to Florida and get that close to Isaiah. Now that I was here, I wanted to look around a bit. I might only remember bits and pieces of my life, but I knew I'd never been here before.

I set my rucksack on the floor.

"I'd like a tour. This is some apartment."

It really was. When I said it looked like a yoga studio, I meant that in the best way possible. How Dice had managed to furnish it like this during the apocalypse was terrific and I could feel the air conditioning on my face.

Dice showed me around the apartment, and I realized it was a hotel suite. Someone had set up an Indian theme hotel, but Dice had gone a few steps further and added his own decoration.

"What kind of hotel is this?" I asked as he led me through the kitchen.

"A Disney themed hotel. Different wings are different countries. A lot of my people are staying here with me. Most of the pilots who will drop the bombs are in this hotel. We repurposed Disneyworld."

"You made Disneyworld your bomb playground?" I asked.

How fucked up was that? It was supposed to be the happiest place on Earth. Dice jumped up and offered me his elbow.

"Welcome to my playground, Speedy Gonzales."

I felt a brief twinge. Someone on my softball team used to call me that. I never knew it was a cartoon character until they showed me a YouTube video. I didn't exactly get to watch cartoons growing up. I wondered where my softball team was now. Were they safe in California or were any of them still alive? Would I even live through this to find that out?

Aeron and Leif got into a little shoving match over who got to take my other arm, but Leif smacked Aeron into a table and snatched up my arm. Dice just cocked an eyebrow at them.

"You're being pretty cavalier with my shit for someone who gets mad at their stuff getting broken."

"Payback is a bitch, isn't it?" Leif grinned.

"One of you is going to have to swap with me later," Aeron said.

The hotel might have power, but we still used the stairs. Dice's hotel room was on the top floor, and there were six floors in this hotel. I knew Dice didn't want to be seen appearing and disappearing in front of his people, so we'd have to take the stairs back up. I didn't mind. I was feeling super out of shape. I'd woken up from that coma, then spent most of my time in San Quintin shoving my face hole with delicious Mexican food. I was finally starting to gain my weight back, but I wasn't precisely in shortstop shape anymore.

The lobby of the hotel was something else. *It had staff.* They weren't in uniform, but there were people at the front desk and the bar. They all waved at Dice when they realized he was back and seemed happy to see him. The lobby of the hotel was posh, and it looked like they made it a point to keep it clean. People were milling about, eating and drinking. They were in regular clothes, but I could tell from the way they held themselves that they were military.

The doors swung open, and we stepped outside. The hotel was actually *in* the theme park. The hotel was still standing, but it looked like a lot of the major attractions had been totally destroyed. A lot of work had been put into clearing the rubble away, and they parked a bunch of planes in their place.

"I thought you were holed up in one of the military bases here?"

"I have apartments all over Florida, but the bombs are here. What better place to hide them? A military base is the first place anyone would look."

"True, but I don't like seeing this place like this."

"It's a travesty, to be sure, but it's needed. We'll rebuild after we beat your father."

"You all seem so sure we're going to beat him. We still have to kill the Rage Heads and get to the White House."

They all just started laughing.

"You seemed to doubt I'd find the serums once I had your blood. You saw how fast I got that solved. Dice can get the bombs ready in that time too. And he's been stockpiling gas for years. So have his people all over the world," Leif said.

"Do we really want to rush the whole bomb thing?" I said. "I think Dice should take his time playing with the explosives."

They were all laughing so hard they were wheezing, and I didn't find the idea of blowing up the entire East Coast the least bit funny. Mostly since I was *on* the East Coast with all the bombs. I was super attached to the idea of not exploding, and I didn't find being in the same area with all the bombs left in the United States the least bit funny.

Dice finally stopped laughing and stared at me.

"I'm an angel, Speedy. I don't do anything so basic like accidentally exploding bombs. If a bomb explodes on my watch, it's because I wanted it to."

I held up my hands.

"Okay, I'm basic when I grab my pumpkin spice latte in certain shoes during the fall. Exploding Florida is so beyond basic, Dice."

Dice held out his pinky.

"I pinky swear not to blow up Florida, Speedy."

"No one is going to blow us up, Ariel," Leif said. "Dice is good at what he does."

"It wounds me you think I'm not."

"If you don't trust Dice, trust us," Aeron said. "We won't let any harm come to you."

I knew that. I knew it like I knew my last name. Still, there were bombs involved. I was starting to feel a little bit better. Dice was an angel. Surely, he knew his explosives. I mean, he hadn't exploded Florida yet. That was a good sign, right?

All three angels snapped to attention.

"Leonard just left D.C. Dice had better get started," Aeron said.

"Did you set up the medical clinic like I asked?" Leif said.

"Yeah, and I promised the people here a vaccine. We've been raiding and hoarding the supplies you asked for, so you'd better come through. Ariel, come with me. I'm going to be teaching you while I play with my bombs."

Okay, that good feeling I had was officially gone. If I didn't even want to be in the same state, I certainly didn't want to be in the same room.

Fourteen

It was so fucked up. Dice's workshop was in the giant castle. The entire bottom floor had been gutted, and there was machinery everywhere now. I was pretty sure this wasn't standard bomb diffusing stuff either. There was a dismantled car engine sitting on the table next to a beat-up couch.

Aeron dragged me over to the couch and flopped down with me. Leif was gone again. Dice showed him where the medical building was, and he disappeared to make vaccines. I missed him, but that was where he was needed. We didn't need our allies revolting because Dice couldn't deliver his promise of a vaccine. Leif kissed me and promised he could duplicate his work in Mexico without my blood. I trusted him. I trusted Dice in this room of explosives much less.

Dice plugged a device into a dock, and music filled the room. He started plugging things into a switchboard on the wall, and things began lighting up.

"Might as well get my radio show back up and running. I've just been playing music and not talking since

I got to Mexico. It's time they heard me again, and now I get to have guests."

"You need to focus on Ariel, Dice."

"I'd rather he focuses on those bombs."

"I can do all three. Smile, you're on the air."

Was Dice seriously controlling all the airways with an MP3 player and a switchboard? How was he doing that, anyway? He flipped a microphone on and sat in front of some weird machinery. He didn't seem to be playing with his bombs yet.

"Ladies and gentlemen, did you miss me? I know I missed you. It's the Horseman of War checking back in. I've got news from across the world! A vaccine for the Rage Mutation should be coming to a city near you, courtesy of the Horseman of Pestilence. Also, pretty soon, you're going to notice things falling from the skies. That's not going to be the only thing dropping.

"When those pretties start dropping, the Rage Heads are going to start dropping dead. Yeah, we've found the perfect solution to mass Rage Head eradication. When I give the word, you want to make sure you stay inside until it's over. And when it's over, you'll need to burn the Rage Heads. We can't afford to bury them. Burn them. Find your loved ones, and put them to rest. It's almost over, folks. Now, enjoy this tune from the Grateful Dead."

Dice started pressing buttons with one hand while fiddling with his engine with his other hand. Music filled the room, and he hunched over his parts with his toothpick in his mouth.

"I thought we were going to be guests on your show?" Aeron asked.

"I thought it was a bad idea to let Isaiah know Ariel was alive. He's already going to know we're working on something to kill his zombie pets. Want to hear his tantrum?"

I raised my hand.

"I would."

Maybe if I heard him again, I'd remember something or at least get some idea of how I'd react when I saw him again. I still didn't know if I'd freeze or lose my shit. When I ran, I never planned on seeing him again. I told myself if he ever came for me, I'd kill myself before I'd let them take me. One of us was going to die when we met again, and I would have four angels as back up. Then again, he would have Satan.

Dice pointed a remote at his docking station. Before he could click a button, I stopped him.

"Hold on a minute. Are you controlling all the radio waves *and* spying on my father from a fucking MP3 player?"

Dice just smirked at me.

"I modified it. See? You don't need to worry about the bombs at all."

"I'm still worried about the bombs, Dice."

Dice just lovingly pat all the parts in front of him.

"This is a bomb."

I recoiled. I hadn't realized I had been sitting so close to it.

"Relax, Speedy. This girl can't go explody anymore. I gave her a lobotomy and took out all her mass destruction parts. Now, I just need to give her a little facelift and move some parts around so she can save the world."

"Your bomb is female?"

"All bombs are female."

"Okay, that's just misogynistic."

"No, hear me out here—bombs end wars. The side

with the most always wins. Only bombs and women have the power to stop wars like that."

"That's totally not true!"

"Hello, Speedy! Horseman of War here. Before bombs, I ended war with the help of women, even during times women weren't given positions of power. Men used to like to think they were keeping women barefoot, pregnant, and in their place, but while men were off misbehaving, I was having tea with their wives. They might not want to listen to me, but sometimes, you don't need to shout loudly to be heard. You need someone trusted to whisper softly. I wish I could still settle wars over tea instead of worrying about bombs. Fewer people ended up dead."

"That's actually beautiful in some weird, fucked up way."

"Do you want to hear more, or do you want to listen to your father have a meltdown?"

"Do it."

I needed to hear it. All the pep talks in the world weren't going to prepare me for seeing him again. All the time in the world probably wouldn't either. I would need as much help as I could get. Dice hit the button on the remote, and the room filled with the sounds of Isaiah's shouts.

"What do you mean you just left? I told you to get your ass to Florida. These men are ruining everything!"

"The man said he was going to kill the Rage Heads. Isn't that a good thing?"

"We talked about this, Leonard. We can't have the Rapture without the Rage Heads. If he destroys the Rage Heads, the Rapture can't happen. Don't you want to be called home?"

"Of course, but so many people have died."

"They were sinners, Leonard. I told you this. The Rage Heads are all sinners. The angels will come and wage war with them. Your job is not done yet. You know what the scriptures say about the Four Horsemen. You know what that man calls himself. You must bring down hellfire on them. Drag as many Rage Heads as you can to their gates and end them!"

"Yes, sir. They must repent or die."

"Remember what I said. Drive straight through any gate or wall you see. If you find a girl with pink hair in the chaos, you steal a car and bring her back here."

"Isn't she a sinner, too, if she's with them?"

"She's the worst kind of sinner, but she's the key to this. I can't have her running around free if she's there with them. Bring her to me if she's there."

"I could use some backup."

"I'll send one of the Bubbas with you. He'll be armed and can cover you when you need to refuel. Try not to piss him off. He's a little ornery."

"Yes, sir. Thank you."

The line must have disconnected because Leonard stopped talking. I heard my father let out a belly roar and the sounds of things crashing around the room. Dice pressed a button, and music filled the castle again.

"Did you want to keep listening to his tantrum?"

"No, that was enough."

Aeron pulled me down to his chest.

"How do you feel, Speedy?"

How *did* I feel? I felt nothing. I wasn't afraid of him. It hit me. *I wasn't scared of him.* He'd been the boogeyman of my bad dreams for so long, and I knew he was the Antichrist now, but I wasn't afraid. Sure, I just listened to him easily manipulate someone into kidnapping me *again*, but I knew that person wasn't going to succeed. I didn't care how many of my father's Bubbas he sent. I wasn't going to end up with him again until I chose to be.

And when that happened, he was going to die.

FIFTEEN

These fucking angels had been laughing about me losing my shit about exploding since Dice got to Mexico, and they only just now decided to tell me Dice had already decommissioned all the bombs, so there was zero chance of wiping the entire East Coast off the map. Honestly, they could have told me that back in Mexico the first time I flipped my shit, and instead, they just had their fun at my expense.

And they were still doing it as I sulked over dinner. I hated being made fun of. Everyone had come together for dinner, and there was this mass cookout. Apparently, outside the theme park, they had set up farms and had fresh vegetables and meat. They didn't get to eat meat unless someone found something on a hunt or an animal had to be slaughtered.

They had to put a pig down, so this guy with substantial mutton chops was supervising a pig roast. It smelled amazing, but I was so mad at these angels for letting the joke go on so long.

Dice plopped down on the picnic table we were sitting

on and started handing out amber bottles.

"Save those bottles when you are done. We try to recycle what we can here, and Stephanie makes the best brew on the entire base. She used wild strawberries in this batch. A peace offering, Speedy?"

"You can't just bribe me with strawberry beer! You all were making fun of me."

Aeron popped the top off his beer with his bare hands. I was trying not to find that so brutishly manly it was sexy, and remember I was mad at him.

"No, we weren't. You were just so adorable when you got worked up about it."

"It's true," Dice said. "I normally wouldn't let it slide when someone questions my work, but your mouth would do this cute little thing when you would start talking about my bombs."

Leif just held up his hands.

"I would like to point out that it was mostly Aeron and Dice. I've been in my lab doing my job."

Aeron ripped the top off one of the amber bottles and set it in front of me.

"We're sorry, Ariel. We weren't trying to make fun of you. We should have told you from the start. You were just so cute. Personally, it meant I could spend more time around you hugging you when you got upset about it."

"I just thought you were cute when your mouth did that thing. I wouldn't have minded getting in on the hug action."

I knew it was probably limited edition, and there wouldn't be seconds, but I chugged half that strawberry beer. I was going to need a slight buzz to explain to these angels why that totally wasn't okay. I slammed the bottle on the table.

"Is this an angel thing? You can't joke about bombs in the middle of the apocalypse because you think my reaction is cute! I don't care what my mouth does when I'm petrified I'm going to get blown to kingdom come."

"You never would have gotten blown up—"

"Which you should have told me back in Mexico!" I yelled.

Leif pulled me into his lap and started playing with my hair.

"You were really scared about that, weren't you?"

I was ready to strangle all three of them, and Leif was really trying to make me feel better. Why was it so shocking that being in close proximity to every single bomb left in the United States and letting an angel who could never bother with a shirt experiment on the explosive part was a little scary? What sane person wouldn't be nervous? In fact, I was a bit worried about being surrounded by a bunch of people who didn't get the fuck out of Florida while Dice was decommissioning the bombs, even if they made delicious strawberry beer and that pig smelled terrific.

"I'm not fucking crazy, unlike the three of you."

"Do you trust me, Ariel?" Aeron said.

"Well, yeah. I wouldn't be alive right now if it weren't for you."

"Do you trust me?" Leif asked.

"Yeah. I trust both of you."

"You agreed to come with me in that hospital with almost no questions asked. After we explained things, you gave Leif your blood because you trusted he could end this with it. I know you don't know Dice as well as you know us, but why didn't you trust us when we said Dice could do everything he promised with his bombs?"

"Because instead of just telling me all the bombs here were decommissioned, you kept up the whole joke because you liked my reaction!"

"No, I mean, even if it were true that there were still active bombs here. You didn't remember me, but I said we needed to go to Mexico, so you followed me. You didn't ask nearly as many questions as someone with no memories should have. I said there was a man you didn't remember in Mexico who could make a cure with your blood. You didn't kick me in the balls and run. You still came. You questioned us about Dice way more than you ever suspected anything about Leif and me.

"It's not just the bombs. You could have died several times over on the road. You could have stayed in the safety of California with Miss Mabel. Leif could have had ill intentions and made things worse with your blood. You trusted us, but you never gave Dice that same trust when we kept telling you that you would be fine in Florida. You trusted us on mostly blind faith."

I gulped. Aeron was right. I had done a lot of crazy shit since I met Aeron. Aeron could have been one of the cannibal rapists in the world, but I left the facility with him. I could have stayed in Gabriel's Haven, but I followed him. I could have stayed behind the walls in California, but I just trusted Leif wasn't going to make things worse with my blood.

Even if they hadn't told me the truth right away, why didn't I accept their answer? I was there when Aeron killed five trucks of Nazis and dazed a ton of Rage Heads so we could kill them with his angel powers. Leif made a vaccine and a killing serum way faster than was humanly possible.

Why did I continuously question that the Horseman

of War couldn't handle bombs?

I mean, Aeron was the Horseman of Death, and I'd seen him in action. Leif was the Horseman of Pestilence, and I was in the lab with him when he had success. I'd seen two Horsemen in action do the impossible. Why didn't I see it before? I was still mad they didn't just tell me, but even if there were active bombs here, the Horseman of War was probably the best person on the entire planet to be fiddling with them.

I totally deflated, and I was about to do something I didn't think I was going to do when I decided to get mad about them not telling me the truth.

"Dice, I'm sorry. I didn't mean to insult you by flipping out about the bombs. I mean, you were able to organize the remaining military to steal them successfully. I should have just gone with that instead of thinking you didn't know what you were doing."

Dice didn't seem to be the slightest bit angry with me. In fact, he wasn't even looking at me. He was eye-fucking that pig roasting on the spit. Okay, that was just insulting. Dice finally started paying more attention to me than the dead pig.

"I'm not mad at you, Ariel. I found the whole thing funny, and it gave us a reason to talk. I guess one of the reasons I didn't just tell you right off is because it meant I got to talk to you more. Sure, you ran to Aeron and Leif for comfort, but it meant you spent more time with me before you went to bed with them."

"It felt weird having you on the couch, even when we first met," I admitted. "It felt like we were leaving you out."

"It meant a lot to me when you invited me, and I hope you don't mind I demanded snuggle time at night."

Did that bother me? It actually didn't. Dice had proved to be this tremendous help getting my memories back, and he was just so easy to talk to. There was something about his appearance that gave off this air of danger, and he *was* dangerous if he could just waltz in and steal all the bombs in an entire country.

Something wasn't right. We shouldn't snuggle in bed at night when we hadn't done something fundamental first. Aeron and Leif had to grab their beers as I crawled across the picnic table and slid into Dice's lap. Every single soldier around us started cheering and hooting. I wrapped my arms around his neck and shoved my boobs as far into his face as I could. His hands snaked around me to cup my ass.

"Well, hello."

"We can't get all cuddly at night until we've had our first kiss."

Dice nuzzled my neck.

"Just in time. The pig is almost done, and I plan on destroying as much of it as they will let me. I wouldn't want to do this with pig breath. We can have a nice strawberry kiss."

"Well, when you put it like that…"

Dice buried his fingers in my hair and pulled me down for a kiss. I forgot about everything around me. It was amazing. It was passionate, and it tasted like strawberries. Neither of us cared a bunch of hooting soldiers surrounded us. The more Dice caressed my tongue with his, the more I wanted him to do the whole angel teleport thing and whisk me back to his bedroom.

Of course, my stomach had to choose right then to go and betray me. Why did food have to happen when I was straddling the Horseman of War? He wasn't anything like

Aeron or Leif, but he had one thing in common with them. As soon as he heard my stomach start screaming, he broke the kiss and was going to make sure I had food.

"How are we coming on that pig? My woman is hungry!" he yelled, smacking me on the ass.

That should have pissed me off, but coming from Dice, it just didn't.

"Carving it up now, boss."

Dice didn't seem to want to let me out of his lap, and I wasn't complaining about that.

"You're in for a treat. Solomon does amazing things with meat and a firepit when we need to slaughter an animal. We found a warehouse that was still pretty well stocked. He combined this and that and made this amazing rub for the pigs. Sarah and James are two of my best pilots, but they grew up on farms. They were able to get so many things growing here, and four of my snipers do beautiful things with fruits and vegetables. Everyone here contributes in their own way, and we have civilians here too who cook sometimes. Stephanie is a civilian, and she's conscripted several for her brewery."

Dice was talking about all the soldiers and civilians here like a proud father. I realized something about him. I knew he was proud of stealing those bombs, so they had no choice but to end the war, but I think he was prouder about all the people that were currently alive and in Florida.

Dice had his crazy side, but he was also a good person. He helped me get back a lot of my memories, and all these soldiers and civilians were alive because of him. I wasn't planning on collecting all of the Horsemen as boyfriends, but as far as falling in love went, Dice was an excellent choice to have that happen with.

Sixteen

Should I have felt the slightest bit weird I just added another boyfriend to my harem and was mowing my way through delicious roast pig in his lap in front of the entire remaining military in the United States? Because I didn't feel weird and no one here seemed to give a shit I made out with their supreme commander but was getting plenty of PDA from Aeron and Leif. It was actually kind of nice that the end of the world meant people were less of judgemental prudes.

I was having a blast. It was easy to forget some awful people destroyed the happiest place on earth, and now it was some sort of military base. The food and company were excellent. I didn't know if they were soldiers or civilians since people were dressed in clothes they could salvage, but there was live music with dinner.

Someone had an acoustic guitar, a violin, and another person had found a tub and was playing the drums. They were good. It could only be original music because the lyrics were all about killing zombies. I may have been fucked in the head, but I was laughing at some of them.

There's nothing quite like a violin wailing while a woman with a snake tattoo around her arms belts out a tune about the crunching sound when you bash a Rage Head's skull in.

We were all fucked in the head because Dice, Aeron, and Leif were laughing too. After we'd totally stuffed ourselves with food, Dice jumped up and asked me to dance. I was a little shocked Aeron got up to dance with us, but totally not shocked Leif did.

Okay, angels were fabulous dancers, and I was having a blast. This was fucking amazing. Dice built something special here. All the settlements I'd been to so far were different. California had high walls and was policed by gangs, but Jade ran a tight ship.

The military now ran Mexico, but Florida was totally different. I hadn't seen a single person in uniform and no guns. Everyone here was relaxed and joking. They were celebrating they had fresh meat and an entire pig this time. From what Dice told me over dinner, people only had meat for dinner if they successfully hunted it or one of the animals had to be put down. If someone success-fully hunted a larger animal, it was shared with as many people as possible.

It was just so fucking nice to be around so many people celebrating. It was also fucking lovely to be smashed between three angels while we danced. I wasn't the only one reacting. My nipples were rock hard, and it wasn't like Aeron and Leif could hide their erections with what they were packing in their pants. A quick glance down confirmed at least three angels I'd met so far had been extraordinarily blessed in the cock department when they were created.

I was trying to make it a point to grind my ass against

all three cocks, and I have to say, I was doing a pretty good job of ass to cock distribution. Aeron was letting out his signature growls, Leif would let out a soft moan, and Dice would straight up smack my ass. My ass was probably covered in his handprints and stinging like fire, but I totally wanted to explore his need to slap my ass repeatedly.

If they weren't going to say anything, I was.

"How about we take the spanking, growling, and moaning back to Dice's room?"

They didn't respond except for a growl, moan, and a spank. I was practically yanked off my feet when two angels grabbed my hands, and they took off running towards the hotel. Dice was hot on our heels. I threw back my head and laughed as we stumbled back to Dice's room like horny teenagers. Okay, most teenagers didn't have foursomes, or that would be totally fucked up. I wasn't even having sex with one person when I was a teenager, much less three.

The angels didn't want to wait on all those stairs. As soon as we got to the stairwell, Aeron practically tackled me and zapped me upstairs. I had to commend him on his aim because the bed was right there. Perfect. I shoved Aeron on the bed. In any normal situation, I wouldn't have been able to push Aeron anywhere, but he knew naked time was coming, so he let me.

Dice and Leif appeared behind and started kissing my neck and shoulders. I tugged at my shirt.

"Help me get this off."

Dice cleared his throat.

"May I have this dance? I'm sure you've got ideas in your head for a group thing, but can I have you to myself for our first time?"

I looked at Aeron, sprawled on the bed. I already knew Leif would be okay with it. Leif went with the flow and seemed okay with anything thrown his way. Aeron was the one who got grumpy about Dice. I thought they had worked their issues out, but that was before I developed feelings for Dice. Was Aeron going to pitch a fit and insist the only way I could be with Dice was if he was with us? He was fine when I was alone with Leif, but there was something about Dice that bothered him.

Or maybe not. Aeron just jumped off the bed and glared at Dice.

"None of your kinky shit."

I smacked Aeron's arm.

"I *want* the kinky shit, asshole. Wait, how kinky are we talking about, Dice?"

"Why? What are your limits?"

"If I see a permanent mark on her perfect skin, I'll rip your fucking wings off," Aeron growled.

I raised my hand.

"Scars are a hard no. No poop, either."

"I'd never defecate on a lady. And I don't leave permanent marks, you winged fuck. You're scaring her. Now, can you run off and kill something so I can be alone with Ariel?"

Aeron looked like he wanted to say something else, but Leif grabbed his arm and steered him out of the bedroom.

"Let's go enjoy the live music and see if there's any more of that delicious pig left. That spinach dish was pretty amazing too."

Aeron just grunted and disappeared. How could they even think about eating again? There were rules about how many helpings of the pig everyone could have, but it was a free for all with the vegetables, and that spinach dish was unlike anything I'd ever had before. There was some sort of homemade cheese in it that was similar to paneer, but it wasn't like an Indian dish. It was something else altogether, and I could have taken a bath in it.

"Do you have a safe word, Speedy?" Dice asked, snapping me out of my daydreams about that spinach.

I actually did because I'd experimented, as any girl should. Every girl should find out if she liked to be tied down and spanked. And I totally did, but finding someone who could do it right always ended up being a total pain in the ass. I'll bet Dice could do it perfectly too.

"Raspberries."

"Good girl. I won't leave any permanent marks. Anything else I need to know? How do you feel about blindfolds?"

I was getting so fucking excited for what was about to happen. I was so glad to hear kink didn't die with half the population. And I was butt crazy about getting tied up, spanked, and fucked by the Horseman of War. If anyone knew how to give a proper spanking, it was probably him.

I ran my fingers down his suspenders and gave them a hard pop against his chest. They were Snoopy today.

"I'm *all* about the blindfolds and being totally restrained."

Dice grabbed his MP3 player and stuck it in another dock. I recognized the music right away, and I already knew what he wanted. *Temptation* by Tom Waits was the perfect song to do a little striptease to. He didn't even have to tell me. I started swaying to the music. Dice flopped on the bed and started rubbing the impressive bulge in his leather trousers.

"Damn, girl. You've had practice," he moaned as I threw my shirt at him.

"A few people from my softball team took an aerobic pole dancing stripping class a few times a week."

"Man, I love California. I can build a pole in here. I'll bet Aeron and Leif would love to view your pole dancing skills."

Maybe, but tonight was about Dice and me getting my ass spanked. I turned around to give him a splendid view of my ass as I slid my trousers down. When I turned around, he was sitting on the side of the bed and crooked his fingers at me.

"How about a warmup spanking? Get on my lap."

Yeah, he totally knew what he was doing. His muscular hand just massaged my ass and thighs for a bit. I was just getting relaxed and turning into a pool of jelly when he brought his hand down. I yelped when I heard the crack of his hand against my flesh and felt the sting. And oh, did it sting in just the right way. It probably left the perfect handprint on my ass.

Dice knew *precisely* how to give a warmup spanking. He didn't just sit there and redden my ass up like an amateur. He built up to it. He gave me breaks where he would massage my ass, or he would slip his fingers between my legs and rub my clit. As far as first-time spankings went, where the fuck had Dice been my entire life? Oh, yeah. Heaven. Could you even do BDSM there? I had questions.

My ass was pleasantly on fire, and I could have done this all night, but I also wanted more. I wanted all Dice had to offer, and I wasn't sure what that was considering it was the apocalypse. I definitely wanted to find out, though.

Dice rubbed my thigh.

"How do you feel?"

I let out a contented sigh.

"Perfect. But I'd feel even better if I was totally tied down and blindfolded. Is that even possible now?"

Dice just chuckled and scooped me up. He gently placed me on the bed and went over to the closet.

"You'd be shocked how many sex shops in Florida were picked over when we decided to make it our home base. One of the local residents is using a four-foot dildo he stole from a shop as lawn decoration. His HOA is all dead, and apparently, they gave him shit about the color he painted his front door. He's got dildos and gnomes all over his lawn now."

"How Florida of him."

"It's actually a thing of beauty. He's got the gnomes worshipping the enormous dildo. The sex shops were picked over, but I can build just about anything."

"I have reservations about homemade dildos, Dice."

Dice just spun around with his hands full of different ropes.

"Why would I make a dildo when I have a cock made by God? I can truss you to that bed and fuck you silly, though."

"Well, what are you waiting for?"

Dice had this shit-eating grin on his face like a kid who walked into a birthday party full of huge presents. He was waving those ropes in the air like a madman.

"Do you want to be on your front or your back?"

"I want more spankings all over, but it sounds like you don't have the toys."

"Ha! Anything is a toy if you're creative."

Dice threw the ropes on the bed and dove back into

his closet. He popped back out triumphantly, holding a ping pong paddle and a thin cane.

"I didn't say we found nothing at the shops. We have a ping pong championship happening on the base, and I'm undefeated. I'll bet this will sting just right on that perky little ass of yours."

He pretty much didn't have to ask me twice. I didn't care about being graceful. I face flopped spread eagle on Dice's bed and waved my red ass at him like it was totally covered in his handprints, and I wanted more. Dice tied me down speedily and like a total pro. I guess the shops weren't totally picked over because he slipped a blindfold over my eyes. I was practically humming with excitement.

Dice actually did start humming and caressed my back.

"I've never had a Nephilim tied down before. Honestly, sometimes I get women who just want their ass tapped twice, and their hair pulled once. They safe word before we've even finished the warm-up and want to get to the fucking. You took yours like a champ."

"I'm not a delicate flower, Dice. The reason I haven't done this more often is that I either met the male version of your female playmates or they weren't real Doms. They just liked hurting women and didn't respect limits or safe words."

Dice was petting my back, and I was practically purring.

"Yeah, not all those assholes turned into Rage Heads. We had to stop a few when we fortified Florida. They hurt some women here, and I broke their faces. Are you ready to play?"

"I want you to show me why you're the ping pong champion of Florida, but all over my ass."

Dice didn't answer. I felt the ping pong paddle come down on my ass. Okay, who knew ping pong paddles felt so delicious on your ass? I had a whole new respect for that game now. I let out a loud moan.

"Oh, my fuck. Ass ping pong is my new favorite game."

"Oh, the Nephilim likes the ping pong paddle. Noted."

Dice slid he free hand between my legs and started making slow circles on my clit while lighting my ass up with the paddle. Holy fuck, I was shrieking and writhing from the pleasure and the pain. It was mingling beautifully that only a talented Dom could bring about.

It didn't take long until my mind slipped off to that special place, and I felt like I was flying. Dice knew precisely how to keep me there too. He didn't say if I needed his permission to come, but he knew when I was about to and kept me right at that fine edge to keep me in subspace as long as possible.

He shifted his hand so he could slide two fingers inside me and still work my clit with his thumb.

"Come for me, little Nephilim."

It was like I shattered into a million pieces. I was a plane, mid-air, that just exploded and fell to earth. I shook and shrieked. My entire body tensed, and Dice knew precisely how to draw out all the little aftershocks.

As soon as my body went limp, he had me untied in no time. I was wrapped up in a blanket and sitting in his lap while he played with my hair. I sighed and just melted.

"You certainly know your aftercare."

"I aim to please. You seemed to like the ping pong paddle too."

"I think bedroom ping pong is my new favorite game."

"If I knew you were into this and we were going to play, I would have made you a handmade flogger."

"Ooh, I love floggers."

Dice just chuckled and started massaging my back.

"I think everyone loves the flogger. I'll make you one when I finished with the bombs."

That was so Dice, and I was starting to appreciate how handy he was with making things. I mean, he was preventing my father from inciting hate groups from an MP3 player. Whatever invention he put on the White House let them hear anything Isaiah said. Hell, maybe I would trust a handmade dildo from Dice.

"That would mean a lot to me, Dice. *This* meant a lot to me. I experimented, but I could never find anyone I could totally trust. It wasn't like that with you, even if you were improvising with the gear. I just knew you'd do it right, and you totally did. That was amazing."

Dice had me tightly wrapped in the blanket and was massaging my shoulders. I just felt *safe*. I had been petrified about coming here because of the bombs, but this was more than just finding out they couldn't explode anymore. This peace had settled over me that I hadn't felt since I woke up in that hospital room. All my doubts were starting to slip away the longer Dice rubbed my back.

We could do this. We could stop Armageddon.

I craned my head up to look him in the eyes. It was a little awkward because he was holding me so tightly it was like he was trying to put me back together after everything that had happened to me.

"What about you?"

"What about me, my lovely?"

"You gave me a beautiful present. Can I return the favor?"

Dice kissed the top of my head.

"You already did. Your submission is a gift, and I'll always treasure it."

I managed to wriggle an arm out and touch his cheek.

"What if I want to make love to you?"

Dice broke into this huge grin.

"Then I would give it to you and say a little thanks to my father for Nephilim stamina. This place is on a backup generator, and I already know how it works, so it's okay if you cause a little power outage. I'd be offended if you don't," he said, nibbling on my neck.

I started wriggling on his lap because his lips felt fucking amazing on my neck.

"I might break your shit."

Angels seemed really offended about shit breakage, and I felt the need to get that out. Dice had me flat on my back in seconds, and his lips found my collarbone.

"I don't care about my shit."

Dice grabbed my hands and pinned them over my head with one hand and started fiddling with his fly with the other. He growled when he realized he had those fucking suspenders on. He snapped them off and shoved his leather trousers down his hips. I wrapped my legs around his waist as he pinned me with his body.

I felt him surge inside me and bit my lip so hard, I tasted blood. Dice kept up this steady, hard pace that was driving me crazy. I couldn't do a fucking thing about it because I was trapped underneath him, but I wasn't complaining in the slightest. I just dug my heels into his ass and moaned. I didn't beg for it harder or faster because I knew better than to top from the bottom. I knew enough about Dice to see that he'd give me what I needed when he thought I needed it.

And oh, did he. Just when I thought I was going to go insane, he started harder and faster. The bed started shaking, and the lights began flickering. Oh, shit, this was totally going to kill me in all the right ways.

"Come now, Ariel," Dice said, speeding up.

It was like I was so conditioned. As soon as he said those words, my world exploded. The lamp across the room exploded, and Dice threw back his head and roared as he came. He gave me a few more hard thrusts before releasing my hands and collapsing on his back. He pulled me to his chest, and I snuggled in.

"How do you feel?"

"Amazing."

"Good, because tomorrow, you're learning how to control the pyrotechnics."

Yeah, we could do that tomorrow. I was fucked out and exhausted. I was passing way out for the rest of the night.

Seventeen

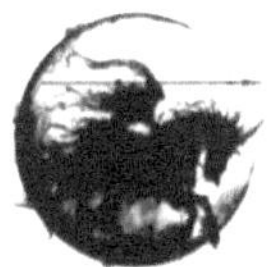

Dice never got out of bed. I woke up smashed between Dice and Aeron. Even though Dice had never gotten out of bed, the power was back on, and the air conditioner was whirring. He didn't mention needing to fix it and kept wanting me to go outside and eat after my shower. I refused to shower with Dice, Aeron, or Leif when there was work to be done. I knew what angels did up against shower walls, and it was seven ways to filthy. We'd never get anything done. However, I did want more shower sex when we weren't busy.

Everyone at the base seemed to eat together at the picnic tables in the middle of the theme park. There was a large fire pit and things to cook on. I wasn't mad about the fact someone made eggs with the leftovers from that spinach dish I liked so much, though I couldn't imagine why there was any left because me and three angels kept going back for more.

I thought fresh bread was a thing of the past. I had pita bread in California, but I was talking about a loaf of fresh sourdough straight out of Miss Mabel's bread maker. Someone brought out toast and homemade butter. I literally almost orgasmed on the spot when I took a bite.

We weren't chatting and having fun over breakfast. We needed to eat and get back to Cinderella's Castle so we could work. I grabbed Leif before he left and pulled him into a kiss.

"I miss you. Am I going to get to see you more soon?"

"Soon, Speedy. I've grabbed a few army medics, and Dice told me where to find a few civilians that can help. My lab here isn't like my one in San Quintin, but it'll do. Do what you need to do."

I knew they needed him in his lab, but I missed my Leif. I held hands with Aeron and Dice as we made our way to the castle. I was in a pretty damned good mood, considering how pissed off I was at dinner. I wasn't as nervous about learning to use my angel grace. No, I was going to master it and blast my father on his ass. I was going to be a total Nephilim badass.

Dice pulled his MP3 player out of his pocket and set it in the dock, but he didn't play music. He put some sort of device over his eye that made his eye the size of a dinner plate and hunched over his pile of parts again.

"Blast that mosaic, Speedy," he said, picking up his screwdriver.

There were still mosaics all over the walls, and I totally wasn't destroying them. Disneyworld might be a military base now, and there might be bombs here now, but some things were sacred.

"No way. I'm not destroying art."

"Hit Aeron then."

"Hey!"

"I'm not hitting Aeron either, Dice."

Dice walked over to a heavy piece of machinery and picked it up like it was a ball of cotton. He walked it to the center of the room and set it down, then went back to his table.

"Are you offended by scrap metal?"

"Cool it, Dice. I didn't want the mosaics destroyed either. It's art. You know she's an amazing artist, right? Look at her arms. She drew those," Aeron said proudly.

Aeron was talking about my sleeves like I was his kid, and I just came home with a picture from school he was going to hang on the fridge. My father pretty much never did that with me, but it was nice to hear Aeron bragging about me like that.

Dice clearly didn't know I'd drawn the art on my arms, even if he knew I was an artist. He looked up from his table, with one of his eyes seriously magnified.

"No shit? I knew you drew, but I didn't know you drew those. Amazing work. How did you tattoo them on yourself?"

"I'm left-handed. I did my right arm, and my business partner did my left and the parts of my right arm I couldn't reach. We have similar styles, and that's why we work so well together. I wonder if they are still alive. Do you know, Aeron?"

Aeron looked crushed.

"I don't. Miss Mabel was able to tell me a few people from your softball team were still alive, but she didn't mention your business partner. A lot of people are still missing. They might be alive and in another state. When the Rage Mutation started happening, people kept thinking there was a safe place to flee. It was the same with the war."

"It's shitty, Speedy. Now, use what you are feeling to move that scrap metal."

I felt this horrible bubbling of shit deep in the pit of my stomach. It was a lot like drinking shitty tequila, trying to eat greasy food with jalapenos to sober up, then changing your mind and drinking again. Imagine that, but thirty minutes later, in the bathroom. That's basically what I felt like after thinking about my business partner possibly being a Rage Head.

I felt Aeron's hands on my shoulders.

"Use what you're feeling," he urged.

I didn't want to use this at all. I wanted to stick my fingers down my throat and vomit it out, even though I wasn't very good at that when I was stinking drunk. I wanted it to go away. But maybe it could. Perhaps I could send it all towards that hunk of sheet metal. I couldn't think of any other way to get rid of it. The only other time I'd used my angel grace was by accident, but I always felt amazing afterward. Okay, most of that was the sex, but maybe I could get rid of this feeling like snakes shed their skin.

I focused on this nasty feeling in my stomach and tried to pull it away from me. I was doing it! My hands started glowing a soft white like Aeron, Leif, and Dice did when we were having sex. I thrust my hands at the scrap metal, and it was like someone shot a bullet at a tin can. There was a spark, and it went flying in the air before it crashed to the floor.

"Ha! I did it!"

Aeron wrapped his arms around my waist.

"Good. Now do it again."

Well, damn. Couldn't he just be happy for me? He was right, though. I needed the practice. I blasted that hunk of metal all around Cinderella's Castle until the screws started coming out, and it was in pieces. It wouldn't do to hit it again. It was dead. I triumphantly killed a piece of scrap metal with my angel grace. Go me!

Dice looked up from his table.

"Excellent work. I also have the answer to kill the Rage Heads. I just need to get my team on it and let everyone around the world know how to do this. Aeron, why don't you take her to eat something? I'll join you soon."

That was the handy thing about angels. *They got shit done.* We were seriously doing this. We were going to stop Armageddon and kill my father.

I was technically now dating three of the Four Horsemen, but they already said Asher wasn't into this, and I wasn't about to have an orgy with the three of them in front of him.

Eighteen

Can I tell you how fucking amazing it was watching people come together after my father tried to destroy the world? Sure, there were still cannibal rapists running around, and Nazis were like cockroaches, and not even the apocalypse wiped them off the face of the earth. But you couldn't keep good people down, and I'd witnessed that in several places now.

Dice hadn't been idle, and he hadn't just ended the war by stealing all the bombs. Florida wasn't only a fortified state and a safe place to live right now. As soon a Dice had a solution to turn the bombs into a solution to kill the Rage Heads, he had a massive team of civilians and soldiers he'd trained to know what the fuck he was talking about when he started giving instruction.

I didn't have the slightest clue how an MP3 player could keep my father from talking to the entire United States or how you could drop bombs around the world and *only* kill zombies, but all these people around us were nodding and high fiving like they totally did. More power to them. I had trouble understanding Ikea furniture instructions, so this was totally over my head.

I lost Dice and Leif after that. Dice had moved out of the theme park to work in large warehouses where they were keeping the bombs. He was where he needed to be, and so was Leif. I wasn't some needy girlfriend that needed to go to work with them, and wasn't that the entire point of having three boyfriends? Aeron didn't need to go around killing anything right now, so we were entertaining each other.

Aeron was one of those angels that didn't like being behind four walls. We were back at the picnic tables, and I was drawing him. Honestly, all of the three Horsemen I'd met so far were so disgustingly beautiful, and I wanted to do nude paintings of all of them. The only reason I didn't have Aeron naked at the hotel so I could sketch him is that I already knew as soon as I got his pants off, he wouldn't behave himself. And I knew I wouldn't either because there was just something super addicting about sex with angels.

As I was sketching Aeron, something was still bothering me, and it grew the more Aeron's visage became visible on my sketchpad. Drawing typically relaxed me, and I went into my own headspace. So, what was bothering me this time? I set my charcoal down and rubbed my face. I was sure I had black smudges all over my face, but that was normal for me when I was drawing.

"What? You aren't drawing me like one of your French girls, and I'm starting to feel self-conscious about it."

"Something is not right."

"Do I need to get naked?"

"No, it's not that."

"Is it a vision?"

A vision wasn't coming on, but that was when it finally hit me. My father locked me in that padded room a *lot* because there was something he wanted me to draw. I was sure there were a few things I drew that he managed to profit from, but maybe that was why he took my memories.

"I think I may have drawn something for my father that he doesn't want me to remember. I rarely got to sleep in my own bed because I was constantly in that padded room. I think there was something specific he wanted to see. I think maybe I eventually drew it, and he wants to make damned sure I don't remember because it could be a game-changer."

Aeron slammed his fist on the picnic table.

"After you kill him, I'm going to kill him again."

"He might know we are coming, Aeron."

"Oh, that's a given. He *knows* we are coming. He would have known that from the start. That was probably part of the reason he raped a Harbinger and had you. It wasn't just your blood. An adult angel would never have cooperated with him, but a terrorized child? You would have done anything he asked, so he didn't hurt you. I'm going to murder that fuck for what he did to you."

"Before you go all murder Horseman, we need to figure out if I drew anything that could help him. I was with him up until my teens, and there's a lot I don't remember. It could be anything."

Aeron grabbed my hand and started marching off towards the hotel.

"Dice keeps a lot of hippy shit in his hotel room that can help you, and we know some Harbingers. Dice isn't the only one who can jog some memories loose."

"I thought you were worried about the whole going crazy thing?"

"And it's still a huge fucking issue. Dice is doing it by focusing on specific topics. That's what we're going to do now."

"What exactly are we doing, Aeron?"

"Some of the Harbingers do this to try to get visions. Like we said, that's all they do. See and witness. It's their entire purpose. Maybe the techniques will help you remember."

"I thought you said I couldn't force a vision."

"Oh, you totally can't. The Harbingers all know that, but they still do this."

"Do what, Aeron?"

He still hadn't told me what we were actually doing. As soon as we stepped into the stairwell, Aeron grabbed me.

"I'm so not doing those stairs."

I didn't want to do the stairs either, but I still wasn't wild about it when they disappeared me places without asking me first. I would have said yes if he asked, but it still irritated me he didn't.

"Can you ask before you just do that?"

"Did you want to take the stairs?"

"No, but you shouldn't disappear and reappear people places without asking them first."

"Sorry. I won't do it again. Let me find Dice's hippy shit. Can you go sit on the bed in Dice's room?"

What the hell. I could just go with this. I didn't need to question everything, and who knew? Maybe this would work. I'd go attempt a handstand naked on the picnic table covered in honey if someone told me it might make me remember something. This wasn't just about feeling whole anymore. If I gave him some crumb that meant we lost, I needed to fucking remember because if we lost, the entire world was going to end. No fucking pressure there, Ariel.

I could hear Aeron destroying things while he hunted down what he needed. I loved Aeron to death, but he could be a bull in a china shop if it meant helping me. Fuck, he'd probably destroy the world himself if it meant keeping me safe.

Aeron came stomping back in with a box and a look on his face like he just won the lottery.

"I'm glad I can always count to Dice to have this shit, even during the fucking apocalypse. He chose this hotel on purpose. Out of all the themed hotels in Disneyworld, this is where Dice feels the most at home. It's fitting for what I'm going to have you do."

"What exactly are you going to have me do?" I asked.

Aeron started setting candles around the room and produced some incense. He sniffed the sticks and scowled.

"I wish Dice didn't like patchouli so much, but it's all we have. It's not like everyone grabbed the incense when they were raiding for supplies, so he actually picked this on purpose. I don't know why he can't go for a nice sandalwood like sane people. We're going to do some guided meditation and see if we can get you remembering if you drew anything."

Okay, that was actually sane and a good idea. So far, Aeron had been more the type to crack my skull open and scoop the portion of my brain out that had the memory if it didn't mean hurting me. Guided meditation with the Horseman of Death. It wasn't the most fucked up thing that had happened to me.

I didn't share his opinion about patchouli, but I

noted not to wear it around him if I could even find patchouli oil anymore. At least I knew I could be stinky around Dice, and he'd love it. Most of the candles weren't scented, but that was okay. They all looked handmade, like someone here was making them for Dice.

Once Aeron had the candles lit, he hit the lights and lit the incense. He climbed into bed and pulled me into his lap. There was just something about being in Aeron's arms where I felt like I could do anything. I sighed and instantly relaxed.

"Close your eyes, Speedy. Focus on your breathing. There's nothing but you and me in this room. Nothing can hurt you here. Memories can't hurt you. No matter what you see, I'm here to keep you safe. I want you to focus on that padded room."

Easy for him to say. That room was a place of terror for me. I never wanted to go back there, but I found myself slipping into what I could remember. He'd lock me in there and come in every night before he went to bed. Isaiah would demand to see everything I drew that day.

He'd shuffle through them and either throw them on the floor or rip them up because they weren't what he wanted. I never knew what he did want me to draw. I just knew whatever it was, I desperately want to do it because he got angry and hit me sometimes if I didn't somehow produce it.

Sometimes, he wouldn't throw a drawing on the floor or rip it up. He wouldn't hit me that time or scream at me. He'd fold the piece of paper and put it in his pocket, but he wouldn't let me out the padded room because it still wasn't right. There was something about the drawing he wanted to keep instead of destroying, but it wasn't the drawing he wanted from me.

I started slipping into a memory. I was close to the age I ran away. I was back in the padded room, and I had a vision. I drew it like always, but when I saw what I drew, I didn't want to give it to him. There were no garbage cans or scissors in the room. There was no place to hide the drawing. I just knew he couldn't see this drawing. I didn't understand it, but I knew it was bad.

There was no place to hide it, so I was going to have to eat it. I'd only torn off one corner of the drawing and was trying to get it down when he barged into the room. I'd forgotten about the cameras in there.

Isaiah ripped the drawing from me, and I cowered. I had no idea why I'd drawn him in the Oval Office with a scary looking angel and four dead angels, but I knew deep down that was what he had wanted me to draw.

He let out this triumphant cry and pocketed the drawing. When he left the room, he didn't close the door and lock it, like I could actually leave and go back to my room now. I knew better. It could be a trick he was using to beat me again. I wasn't leaving my padded room until he told me out loud it was okay. I grabbed my blanket and pillow and went to sleep on the floor like I always did.

I started planning to run before I fell asleep. Whatever that drawing meant, I knew I needed to be as far away from him as possible when it came true.

I gasped and tore myself away from the safety of Aeron's arms to look him in the eyes. Because even though I drew them face down and couldn't see what they looked like, I knew who those four dead angels were now. I was practically hyperventilating.

"I drew you *dead* with I think Satan and Isaiah standing over your dead bodies! That's what he wanted me to draw in that room. That's what he didn't want me to remember. He *wants* you to come to him because he's going to summon dear old dad to kill you!"

Aeron grabbed me and jerked me back to his lap.

"Think, Speedy. That was the vision decades ago. We have put things in motion to change that. He doesn't have you prisoner to warn him when we are coming anymore. He doesn't know about the second painting where he's dead, and we're all fucking over his dead body."

"How does that work if I've painted two different endings to the end of the world? I thought Harbinger's visions always come true? That's not really possible if there's the real ending, then the director's cut alternate ending."

Aeron kissed the top of my head.

"I love that you turned that into a movie reference. That's easy. Think about the Nazis. You changed that vision because you warned us, and we got involved. A lot of different decisions changed the drawing you gave Isaiah. You ran, we reached out to you, you decided to work with us. We aren't dying, Speedy, but that orgy is totally happening."

I felt sick to my stomach, and I couldn't say a damned thing about the orgy this time. What Aeron said made a lot of sense, but it still didn't make me feel better.

I was way less gung-ho about ending up at the White House and killing my father.

Nineteen

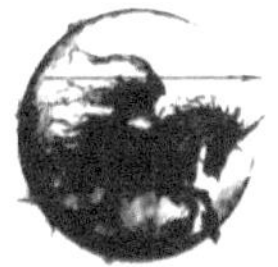

That horrid bad tequila and jalapenos feeling in the pit of my stomach was back, and it didn't matter what Aeron, Dice, or Leif said to me. Dice and Leif came back around dinner, and we were back at the picnic table. We weren't getting a pig roast again, but there was some sort of stew. Dice said it was rabbit. I'd never had rabbit before, but it wasn't half bad, even if it was light on the meat. There were plenty of potatoes and vegetables to fill me up.

"We aren't going to die, Ariel," Dice said.

"It's true," Leif said. "We might have if Isaiah had wiped your memories and kept you in D.C. with him to warn him we were coming, but he made a massive mistake keeping you in that coma trying to tweak the Rage Mutation. I hate to say this because both scenarios are awful, but if he wanted to make absolutely sure that painting was going to come true, he should have wiped your memories and pretended like you didn't know him so you would help him."

That just made me feel even worse. Either situation

was fucked up, but it would have been even worse if I had been back with him helping him because I couldn't remember. Would it have even gone down like that? He couldn't pretend around me forever. He'd have some sort of meltdown about something, and I'd see him for what he was. Even if I didn't remember who he was, I'd know he was a bad person.

It would have been like growing up with him all over again, except now he was President and had men with guns doing his bidding. He had my fear and that padded room when I was growing up, but he wasn't above letting every single one of those men rape me just to keep me in line.

I let out a shaky breath.

"Guys, this is the shittiest pep talk you've given me so far."

I was suddenly enveloped in some massive three-part Horseman hug, and they were squeezing me so tight, I almost couldn't breathe.

"How can we make it better, Speedy?" Dice asked.

"I have no idea. You all say my paintings always come true. I know it makes sense that I later drew us winning because of the decisions we all made, but I don't know how all this works. What if we do something or Isaiah does something that makes the first drawing come true?"

I pressed my face into Leif's chest, but he pulled back a little and tilted my chin up to look him in the eye.

"Ariel, do you have a clear memory of the first drawing?"

"I wish I could forget it. Satan is horrible."

"I know. Forget him. Were *you* anywhere in that drawing?"

"No, I wasn't. The Oval Office was totally trashed.

There were walls completely smashed through, and it broke all the windows. The furniture was all totally destroyed. There were four men dead on the floor. I knew they were angels because their wings had been ripped off and were scattered around the room.

"I knew this was why he had built that padded room and locked me in there, but I didn't want to draw anything else that could help him make it happen. I started plotting to run after that. I started stealing things Isaiah wouldn't miss, but people would pay a lot of money for at school. I built up a little nest egg and ran when he couldn't watch me. I was in gym class and said I really had to go to the bathroom. I grabbed my gym bag out of my locker, put a hoodie on, and walked to the bus station. I was terrified, but I got away."

"Don't you see, Ariel? If you hadn't run, we would never have gotten close to you. We wouldn't have your blood to create the vaccine or the kill serum. Things would have been totally different when we confronted Isaiah. We wouldn't have waited to take him out because we were trying to find you. Isaiah would be the one with a Harbinger in his pocket, not us. You running changed everything!" Leif said.

"No way. You're full of shit, Leif. I didn't change the entire fate of the world because I ran away."

Dice spun me around and looked me dead in the eye.

"Not alone, but you set things in motion. Isaiah made decisions too that sealed his fate, as did all of us. Isaiah saw your drawing and assumed he had already won, so he didn't look for you and bring you back home. Aeron and Leif could have left you in peace since you didn't live with him, and everything on paper said you were estranged from him. They decided to get close to you, and that brought you to us. Fuck, even Satan himself, made some grave decisions. He followed Isaiah's lead when he was summoned because they were both going off *your* first drawing. It's kind of beautiful if you think about it. A huge fuck you to both of them after what they did to you."

I was perking up a little bit and feeling slightly better. I dragged my toe on the ground and bit my lip. I was totally acting like a child, but this was all a little too much.

"Did I really fuck over Satan?" I pouted.

The pep talk totally changed gears. They were all enthusiastically nodding their heads.

"Totally," Leif said.

"You ruined centuries of planning, Speedy," Aeron said.

Dice just cracked up laughing.

"I'd love to see ol' Lucifer's face when Isaiah gets sent straight to Hell, and he realizes he *didn't* win after all this shit."

Aeron started giggling.

"Oh, my god, he's going to have one of his meltdowns. I'd pay good money to watch that if you could get Satan Meltdowns on pay per view."

Leif let out a belly laugh.

"If you think Isaiah can pitch a tantrum like a toddler, he's got *nothing* on Satan. Speedy, if it makes you feel any better, Satan is going to blame Isaiah for this going ass up at the last minute. Hell is not a pleasant place, especially if Satan has a personal beef with you. He won't care Isaiah is his son. We're talking eternal torture here."

I broke into a gigantic smile. Shitty mood? Totally gone. I was still thinking about all the scenarios where things could go wrong in the Oval Office, but when you found out you personally fucked over Satan himself and your stupid father had some eternal torture coming his way, you just had to smile.

"Thanks, guys. We should totally celebrate fucking over Satan."

All three angels broke into grins. That was what I loved about them. Whatever came out of my mouth, they'd be totally up for it, no matter how insane it was.

"What did you have in mind, Speedy?" Leif asked.

I wasn't in the mood for crazy unless you counted taking on three naked angels totally insane, but no one who knew me could say I had a sane bone in my body. I was always fucking up and doing stupid shit. But hey, I did at least two things right. I got away from my father and trusted Aeron and Leif after I got to know them.

I gave them an evil grin.

"All of us, naked and together."

They started dragging me towards the hotel. Yeah, always up for anything.

TWENTY

Can I say I was super proud of all three angels that we were all tripping over ourselves to get back to Dice's room and get naked, but when we got to the stairwell, they all stopped and asked me before they just zapped me up to the bedroom? I said yes, and I probably always would. I had no idea why I wanted to die on this hill about not popping me places with angel powers, but it bothered me. No one ever said I had logic.

I was in the bedroom in seconds, but I was so offended I still had clothes on. I started tearing off my clothes and looked towards my angels.

"Naked, now!"

Dice just frowned at me.

"Easy, Speedy. You've never had three angels before. We've never shared a woman before. Down and dirty has its place, but not in a foursome."

"I know. But I want to roll around naked and have a filthy angel make-out session on your bed."

"In that case..." Dice said, ripping his suspenders off and going for his fly.

Someone tackled me from behind and flung me on the bed. I fell out laughing and already knew it was Aeron. Leif hopped into bed and started kissing my neck. Don't ask me how they got naked before Dice since Dice always wore fewer clothes. Dice stood at the foot of the bed with his hands on his hips.

"Well, shit. That's *my* bed, you know."

"Gotta be faster when she asks you to get naked," Aeron said, sucking on my nipple.

Dice just went angel bowling and dove in the center of the bed. He was right on top of me. Aeron growled when Dice elbowed him in the face, and Leif grunted when he took an elbow to the ribs.

"Asshole," Aeron growled. "Quit hogging Ariel. And keep your elbows to yourself."

"Dick move, Dice," Leif said.

"Don't get your angel panties in a twist. I just want a kiss, and then I'll be moving much lower since both of you are ignoring the pleasure zone. More for me."

"Okay, if this White House orgy actually does go down like all of you keep saying, how do you expect to accomplish that if we can't even start a naked make-out session?"

Dice placed his finger over my lips.

"The White House orgy is going to be perfect. This is just a minor hiccup. I told you, we've never shared like this before. Give us time to work out the kinks. Now, shut up and kiss me."

Dice didn't even give me a chance to respond. He kissed me so hard, I was panting, then he just fucking stopped and pulled away.

"Proceed, gentlemen. I'm moving towards greener pastures."

Dice was throwing elbows again as he climbed down my body. Yeah, first time foursomes were awkward at first, but when Leif and Aeron realized where Dice was headed, they just shrugged and acted like they weren't pissed at him for jumping on me. I'd pretty much never be mad at one of these angels jumping on top of me.

I didn't even want to think about their little spat anymore because Aeron had his tongue in my mouth, and Leif was doing things to my tits that were nowhere near angelic. Dice was between my legs, lapping at my clit. Oh, shit. Almost every erotic area on my body was getting attention between hands and mouths. They were like angel spider monkeys, and I loved every minute of it.

My back practically arched off the bed when Dice slid two fingers inside me, and Aeron started focusing on my neck. Leif was showing my breasts so much attention, they were becoming extra sensitive. I was totally delirious, and we had barely even gotten started. My hands groped for the nearest cock. I wrapped my hands around Leif and Aeron's cocks and started stroking. They both responded the same—they bit me.

Aeron took his teeth out my neck and looked down at our tangled bodies.

"Please tell me someone is prepared for this. Do we have lube?"

"I brought mine," Leif said.

"Regular or edible?" Dice asked.

Since we were stopping, I had questions.

"I thought you said they picked the sex shops over? How the fuck did you find edible lube?"

"I have my ways. Aeron, be a peach and fetch the lube."

"Fuck you. You get it."

"Oh, shut up. I'll get it," Leif said. "I'll just grab mine since I know where it is."

I touched his cheek.

"I adore your angel pockets, Leif."

I shrieked when Dice hauled me up and placed me on all fours. Of course, since my ass was right there, he gave it a hard smack.

"Give Leif and Aeron's cock some attention while I prepare you, Speedy."

Well, there *were* two massive cocks *right there.* I wasn't about to argue. I wrapped my hand around Aeron's cock and started stroking, then gave Leif's a long lick. Leif and Aeron let out little groans and just lounged on the bed with their hands behind their heads like cats with milk.

Dice was pretty much doing amazing things to my ass, and I tried to remember how much attention Leif and Aeron had shown me earlier tonight. No, how much attention they *always* showed me. Nothing says I love you like a blowjob, right? There were plenty of ways for me to show them I love them, but tonight was all about the blowjobs.

I had a dick buffet to choose from, and I was trying to give Leif and Aeron equal attention. I always wanted each of them to feel like they had a special place in my heart because they did. Even if circumstances had me spending time with some of them more than the others, I never wanted anyone to feel left out.

I cherished all of Leif's moans and Aeron's little growls. I loved it that I could make Aeron totally lose control. I loved the fact that Dice would never lose it with me. Leif could go either way and could meet whatever mood I was in and I was totally here for that.

Dice checked in on me. Dice would always check on me before proceeding to the next step.

"How are you feeling, Speedy?"

Honestly, I was perfect. I had Leif's cock in my mouth and was stroking Aeron with my hand. Dice was doing things behind me that had my body singing. I could have done this all night, but I knew communication was important, so I took Leif's cock out my mouth and gave him an answer.

"Pretty fucking amazing," I sighed.

Dice pet my back, and I practically started purring.

"Amazing enough to continue?"

"Oh, yeah. You're pretty talented with the whole warmup thing."

"You should see me end wars," Dice bragged. "Can we do this without fighting? I'd like to claim Ariel's ass."

I was all fucking for that, but *could* we do this without fighting? I pretty much knew Leif would go with the flow because he always did. Could Aeron do this without arguing with Dice? Apparently so because Aeron totally shocked me.

"I want more of that delicious mouth."

I didn't peg Aeron for casting himself in a role where he would be passive and at my mercy, but I was already thinking about all the things I could do to him. Aeron just gave me a gift because he was a bit of a control freak, to put it mildly.

Dice decided to Dom the entire room and made sure everyone was totally okay with what we were doing. I didn't know how Leif and Aeron felt about it, but it just warmed me towards Dice because it only cemented it in my head that he would never take things too far and seriously hurt me.

"Are you okay with the arrangement, Leif?" Dice asked.

Leif just gave me a crooked smile.

"I'm satisfied with just a smile from Ariel."

That was so Leif and totally the perfect thing to say. Leif always managed to find the right words. I climbed up his body so I could kiss him. I pulled away and touched his cheek.

"You're perfect, Leif."

"Of course, I'm not going to complain when you're naked and throwing a foursome my way either. You're the most beautiful thing I've ever seen when you're naked."

"Compliments? How dare you. How did you know that's my weakness? I'm already naked, champ. You don't have to kiss my ass to get my clothes off. Why don't you climb to the edge of the bed?"

Leif was totally adorable, and I realized something about Aeron. As much as he traded barbs with Dice, he didn't say a single word to Leif when he took his elbow to his ribs. He just let out a grunt. He would and did say something when Dice did the same thing. I liked it that both Aeron and Dice were more agreeable to Leif than they were with each other because Leif was one of the kindest people I'd ever met.

And I totally intended to ride him like one of those mechanical bulls.

We were going to have to work out what to do with our elbows during orgies because I got both Aeron and Dice with mine when I was trying to mount Leif. They didn't say a damned thing, but as soon as Leif was buried to the hilt inside me, Dice tangled his hands in my hair and gave it the most delicious pull. He yanked me, so he pressed my back against his chest, and bit my neck.

"Remember, Speedy. I'm the only one allowed to assault Aeron."

"Asshole. I'll kick your fucking ass," Aeron growled.

Leif just tightened his fingers on my hips.

"Guys? We're in the middle of an orgy. Ain't nobody got time for you to take a break for one of your epic fistfights."

Were they seriously going to do this with Leif deep inside me and Dice pulling my hair like a pro? Dice chuckled right in my ear, and I broke out into goosebumps.

"Aeron and I have beaten each other up over some petty shit, but never a woman, and we aren't going to fight now. Right, Aeron?"

"I always want to punch that mohawk straight off your head, but not right now."

This was so fucking awkward, and I couldn't move a muscle because of Dice's hold on me.

"Is the shit officially dealt with?" I asked.

Dice shoved me down, so we pressed my chest against Leif's.

"Game on, Speedy."

Well, it was about damned time. Now that we'd all elbowed each other a few times and decided not to have some angel throwdown, they weren't wasting any time. I felt cool lube squirt down my ass, and Dice started pressing forward. Leif was writhing underneath me in the most remarkable ways. Aeron was just watching, and that was totally not right.

"Aeron, what the fuck are you doing? Get over here."

Aeron was transfixed and not getting over here and putting his cock in my mouth like he volunteered for.

"I didn't think I would like watching this so much.

This is a tremendous turn on."

"You're such a pervert. I love it. How did you want to play this, Death?"

Aeron leaned into the pillows and grabbed his cock.

"I think I want to enjoy the show for a little while before I join in."

"Kinky. I love it. I—"

I couldn't finish my sentence. I let out this massive moan because Dice's hips met my ass, and I had all of him. I'd done this before with Aeron and Leif, but it felt different this time. The pleasure and pressure were there, but I had the added sensation of Dice pulling my pulling my hair, and when I said this angel knew the mechanics of a proper hair pull, it was probably one of the most accurate things I'd ever said in my entire life. He managed to do it, so it stung just right but didn't rip out any of my hair and managing to figure out that balance was some kind of witchcraft.

Aeron was watching us like this was the best movie he'd ever seen in his entire life, and he'd be dropping quotes from our orgy like he did with his favorite movies. His hand was wrapped around his thick cock, and he was slowly stroking it. His pupils were so blown out, his eyes looked black. Yeah, Aeron was undoubtedly enjoying himself, and I intended to give him a little show until he decided to join in.

I looked down at Leif. His eyes were hooded, and he was digging his fingers into my hips. I buried my face in his neck and gave him a few love bites. He moved his hands from my hips to wrap them around my waist and thrust up harder. Exactly what I wanted.

I started riding Leif's cock and slamming back against Dice. If I thought Dice knew how to pull hair before, he upped the ante when I egged him on and left a perfect handprint on my ass.

Aeron was super anti me getting hurt in any possible way. If 911 were still a thing, he probably would have called it if I got a papercut. Aeron was shocking the shit out of me tonight because both of us let out this big moan when Dice spanked me. Aeron didn't threaten to beat the shit out of Dice. No, he was totally digging this.

My eyes snapped up to meet Aeron's. His eyes bore into mine, and the corner of his lip crooked up in a smile.

"Mind if I join in? I may literally explode if I don't."

"No exploding in my bed," Dice grunted, slamming into my ass.

"Get over here and get your cock in my mouth, Aeron."

Aeron was the only one of us that hadn't thrown an elbow at anyone yet, but he did knee Leif in the head trying to get situated. This was kind of like the roller derby version of an orgy the way body parts kept colliding. But we were still working out the kinks of having a foursome, and we had time to figure out how to do this without maiming each other.

I took Aeron in my mouth, and I should have known he had no intention of being passive while this was going down. I had to relax my throat because he was fucking my face pretty hard. There was nothing wrong with a good face fuck if done right, and in this setting, it was totally right.

I was entirely at the mercy of these three angels, so I relaxed and surrendered control. I held onto Leif for dear life and just enjoyed the ride. And a foursome with three of the Four Horsemen of the Apocalypse was better than any ride in this destroyed theme park. I mean, I'd never been to Florida or Disneyworld to compare notes, but I could safely say spinning teacups had nothing on getting fucked like this by all three of them at once.

They totally wore me out before they let go. I'd lost track of how many times I came. I was shaking and clutching Leif when I guess they must have used that whole angel radio thing to talk to each other and agree the orgy was over because they came one right after the other like they fucking planned it. I wouldn't put it past Dice to be orchestrating the entire thing psychically until he thought he'd gotten every last orgasm out of me, and I couldn't handle anymore.

We collapsed into a heap, and I snuggled into Dice and Aeron.

"How are you, Ariel? Was it too much?" Dice asked.

I sighed. I was fucking exhausted and aching in such a good way. This is how everyone should feel if you've been fucked properly, and I certainly had been.

"It was so perfect, and I can hardly keep my eyes open."

Aeron just chuckled and kissed the top of my head.

"Sleep, Speedy, because we are going to do this again."

"Promise?" I yawned.

"We're so going to do this on the desk in the Oval Office to celebrate killing your father."

I just grunted and closed my eyes. It was getting harder and harder to deny that Oval Office orgy was going to happen. I pretty much fell for Dice and had an orgy with three of them. I didn't know the first thing about Asher, and by all reports, he wasn't down for having sex with me either.

Still, something seemed to be drawing me towards the Horsemen if I was now dating three of them.

Twenty-One

I didn't remember a lot of my life, but between Dice and Aeron, I remembered more. Sure, there were still bad people out there, but I honestly couldn't remember people coming together this much before the world went to shit. Sure, if there was a disaster, people forgot their differences and tried to work together to fix things, but this was an extended disaster. I'd been to Gabriel's Haven, California, Mexico, and now Florida. We met some bad people on the road, but the only arguments I'd seen and people threatening fistfights were Aeron and Dice.

I'm sure there were arguments in the privacy of people's homes, but for the most part, Florida was all working together to get those bombs and planes performing to kill the Rage Heads. They'd managed to scrounge up satellite phones, and there was constant chatter all around the theme park from all corners of the world. It was pretty amazing. There was either one person there who spoke English who could translate or someone here who could.

It was finally coming together, and we were celebrating minor victories. Dice had trained a shit load of soldiers and civilians in his odd methods of techno hacking. I was convinced Dice was some kind of angel MacGyver and probably could have built something to kill the Rage Heads with a tin can and one of his toothpicks.

There were so many people here, and Dice ran a tight ship. I felt like I should have a job because everyone else did. Aeron walked around, asking if we could help people because I wanted to contribute. People let me try to be nice.

I learned the hard way farm animals fucking hated me. Cats and dogs always loved me, but livestock was an entirely different story. I was now totally on board with Aeron's theory that chickens were evil velociraptors with no soul. I couldn't even help collect eggs because they ambushed me with those nasty beaks.

I was high tailing it out a chicken coop with hay in my hair, bleeding peck marks, and broken egg goop on my clothes. Aeron refused to set foot in the enclosure and was waiting for me when I got out.

"See? Straight up evil mini dinosaurs."

I pulled a piece of hay out of my hair.

"Okay, that was totally unprovoked. It was like they took it personally I was harvesting the eggs. How do humans have like, a million egg recipes, and put it in so many foods if they fight back when you try to get their eggs?"

Aeron just ran his fingers through his hair and led me away from the coop.

"Have you noticed none of the farm animals here like us? It's always been like that. We draw some animals to us, and others don't want to be around us. We've never figured out why. You know how much Meremoth scares you when you're on his back? Being on a regular horse is so much worse. They don't obey us and want us off their back. We don't generally use regular horses, but one time, Dice and I got called, and this general insisted his warhorses were better than ours, and we couldn't fight by his side unless we used his. Cluster fuck doesn't even begin to describe it."

"Why didn't you warn me before I tried hanging out with cows and chickens, Aeron? Those chickens tried to eat me!"

"I wasn't sure if it would be the same for you since you're a Nephilim, and it seemed important to you to help out. Maybe you don't need to farm or tend to the animals. Art is still essential, Ariel. Never think it isn't just because of what's going on. There needs to be a record of everything that has happened and everything that was done. People aren't exactly taking photos anymore.

"You've been a lot more places than most people have since all this started. You've seen Gabriel's Haven, California, Mexico, and now Florida. You've seen the good and the bad in people. I know there was a lot you missed, but you're witnessing history. You were there when the vaccine was made, and you'll be there when the modified bombs.

"You're an amazing artist, Speedy, and you should draw what you've seen for historical purposes. It's going to take time for things like the internet and publishing to come back. By the time it's back up, memories won't be fresh. Things will get embellished. People who didn't see what you have seen will write about things they only heard secondhand. Draw and paint history, Speedy. The apocalypse still needs artists."

I flung myself at Aeron so hard, he practically fell over. I wrapped my arms and legs around him like a spider monkey and kissed him with everything I had. That was pretty much exactly the right thing to say, and I loved him for it.

My only actual skills were drawing, sarcasm, I had an excellent throwing arm, and I could hit a curveball. The throwing arm and curveball thing came in handy for bashing in zombie's brains, but painting and a potty mouth weren't exactly survival skills.

In Mexico, I knew my actual job was getting my blood to Leif, but I had hard drives I could go through to contribute in my own way. I didn't have that in Florida, and I was feeling self-conscious I was the only one not working. No one said anything to me about it, and it honestly felt like they were humoring me when they did let me help, but it was shit that had been running around my head on repeat.

I'd always been proud of my art, and I'd managed to turn it into a pretty successful career. Sure, the drawings I'd done since I woke up from that coma had saved some lives, but I kept telling myself they didn't count. I didn't have a choice about those drawings. Aside from sketching Aeron, I hadn't sat down and drawn anything just for fun or to make some statement I wanted to make since I left that research facility.

Aeron was right. I'd seen some shit, and I could document it. I hadn't seen a single person with a camera in any of the places I'd been, even the ones with working electricity. That didn't mean there weren't people documenting things and trying to store them on a laptop if they managed to find one, but I'm sure SD cards were scarce, and hard drives eventually got full.

"Have you been taking cues from Leif? That was exactly the right thing to say."

Aeron cupped my ass and started walking back towards the hotel.

"I've been known to sometimes make a good point. Let's see if we can get you some supplies. Dice probably scavenged some because he knew you were coming. I expect a huge painting of me on top of Meremoth with the sun shining out my ass."

"Am I allowed to paint those big, sexy wings of yours? I might want that one for the bedroom."

"In that case, I'll pose nude."

I moaned at the picture in my head of Aeron, sitting naked on his murder horse with his wings out.

"I'd never get anything done."

Aeron just chucked.

"That's the idea. Let's go find you some supplies so you can get famous documenting history, Speedy."

These were probably going to be the most important paintings I'd ever done in my entire life, and they didn't involve painting the future.

Twenty-Two

Can I say I can't believe I used to be uncomfortable around Dice? Aeron found an entire stash of paint in his hotel room, and it was the good shit too. It was the type of paint I'd spend a whole paycheck on. Paint wasn't exactly a desirable item for scavenging during the apocalypse, and he had an entire rainbow of colors. He snagged a few canvases and canvas making supplies too.

People had been humoring me when I asked to help, but now they were super curious when I was out by the picnic tables building canvases and painting. They all wanted to know what I was doing and wanted to make sure I painted them right.

I hadn't gotten to Florida yet. I'd started painting what I could remember about Gabriel's Haven. I figured I should start from the beginning because those memories were going to fade first.

It was pretty great. No one in Florida had heard of it, so they stopped to ask me. It allowed me to talk to people and make some friends other than my three angels.

I was happily going about my business working when Aeron just casually dropped a bomb.

"So, Ariel. Want to take a break and go kill Leonard and Beavis?"

"I thought it was a random Bubba. Wait. What?"

"Asher reported in. Leonard and Beavis have made it to the New Jersey sign like in your painting. We decided to go to New Jersey and kill them. Want to come?"

"You say that like we are going to the mall, and it's not the apocalypse."

Aeron just shrugged.

"Going to the mall, killing Beavis and Butthead. It's all the same to me."

"Can I clean my brushes, then we leave?"

"Excellent."

I got everything cleaned and put away. Dice and Leif met us at the hotel. I wondered if I was going to meet the mysterious Asher in New Jersey. Dice pulled out a laptop and started clacking on the keys. How were we even going to find these guys in all of New Jersey? Was New Jersey some sort of safe haven like California, Mexico, and Florida? I was sure they would object to a politician and a redneck dragging zombies to their state. I was pretty sure that sentence could only ever be uttered during the apocalypse or a really fucked up zombie movie, but here we were.

"Are we just going to walk around the entire state of New Jersey until we come across an RV making a lot of noise?" I asked.

Dice just scoffed.

"You should know me better than that by now, Speedy. We're going to land right on top of that RV, and I made a new toy to kill the stragglers."

"I get you're angels, and you have all these superpowers, but they could be fuck all anywhere by now. My visions aren't exactly precise, and Asher just said he overheard a phone call where Leonard was checking in at the New Jersey state line."

They all just started laughing, and I fucking hated when they did that. They were about to angelsplain some superpower about how it would work, but I had no fucking way of knowing that, and they didn't have to laugh about it. I didn't know how shit went down in Heaven, but on Earth, it was considered gauche to make fun of someone who had lost their memories and didn't know something.

I was going to say something. Just because they were fucking angels didn't mean they could laugh at me when they felt like it. There were times when it was totally appropriate to make fun of me for something because I earned that shit, but not knowing something? That was never appropriate. I don't give a shit if you were created fully formed by God and managed to save the world several times over.

"Okay, it's totally not okay to laugh just because I don't know something. You do that shit a lot, and most of the time, even if I had all my memories, I'd have no fucking way of knowing what you were about to tell me that you think is hilarious I don't know. That's a dick move, even for humans."

Every angel in the room had the decency to look adequately chastised, but it was Leif who pulled me in his lap and spoke. Of course, Leif was going to be the one that tried to diffuse things when I got pissed off with them.

"We're not trying to make fun of you, Ariel. You just

fit in so well with us that it's like you're the fifth Horseman. We aren't laughing because we're making fun of you. It just hits us when you question us like this that you *haven't* been with us since they created us.

"It's unfair. I know we are angels, and we are supposed to be all about our jobs. But why didn't someone like you come along before now? It's not just that you're a Harbinger, and we could have used the help of one this entire time. We didn't know we needed a tattoo artist with pink hair who could get all our personal quirks as you do."

"We aren't laughing at you for asking questions, Speedy. It just hits us when you do that you haven't been with us forever, and the only thing we can do is laugh because it's unfair. We're constantly getting called to Earth to save it, but no one ever knows, and we never get any thanks. Why did it take the Antichrist kidnapping, raping, and killing an angel for us to find love?" Aeron said.

"We've spent a lot more time on Earth than a lot of angels, Ariel. I think you've seen by now that there's a lot here that we love. But we've never been *in* love before. We avoided it because it never made sense before. It does with you, and it's deeper than your paintings. But yeah, we think it's unfair and can't figure out why our father didn't create you for us. The only thing we can do it laugh about it. But yeah, it totally feels like you've always been with us, and it's fucking weird when you don't know something," Dice said.

"You think all of this shit hasn't been totally weird for me? That's why I keep asking questions and getting pissed when you laugh at me!"

"Speedy, we aren't making fun of you for not knowing something, I swear. To answer your question, I can get an exact location on Leonard and the redneck from his satellite phone. I can hack anything given enough time, and I've already been watching the satellite phones Isaiah handed out. Once we make sure you're happy again, we can go kill Leonard, Bubba, and some zombies."

I sulked like a total teenager. I got their explanation, but it still felt like they were making fun of me.

"Killing things *would* make me feel better."

Leif played with my hair.

"Do you want to go kill an extra Bubba right this minute, or did you want to talk things out?"

"I guess I get it, but I don't feel better."

"Let me try to explain then," Leif said. "We were created around the same time man was kicked out of the Garden. Scientists absolutely got evolution correct, and their estimated age for the world is almost right. Seven days moved a lot different then. That should give you an idea of how old we are and how long we've been doing this. It should also tell you how long it's just been the four of us.

"We've been stopping plagues, wars, warlords, megalomaniacs, and the Antichrist since people were grunting and living in caves. We've only had each other's company that entire time. It never made sense to date a human. Angels aren't given the knowledge of knowing where they end up when they die, and humans aren't always honest. We never wanted to risk falling in love with someone and then having them ripped away from us when they died."

I held my hand up.

"Hold on a minute. My dad is the fucking Antichrist, and my past isn't exactly lily-white. I'm pretty sure I've hit all the major sins, whether on purpose or by accident. I didn't technically know that guy was married at the time.

If you want to get even more technical, I've committed murder too, though I don't know if Heaven is going to hold it against me that everyone I've killed so far was a Rage Head or a rapist. Is someone going to get mad if I kill Leonard and this random Bubba? How do you know I'm not just going to end up in Hell with the rest of my family?"

Well, this conversation just took a turn for the worse. Now, I wasn't just upset about getting laughed at. I was scared about the future of my eternal soul. I'd fucking celebrated screwing over Satan because I wasn't thinking about what was going to happen when I finally kicked the bucket. He was probably going to take it personally I helped fuck this up for him.

They didn't laugh this time. They all just started trying to assure me I wouldn't all at once.

"If you don't know where people end up, how do you *know?* My heritage is pretty fucking bad, guys."

"You forget your mother because you never met her. No one with angel blood has ever ended up there in the entire history of the world *except* the Antichrist and the fallen," Aeron said.

"That doesn't make it better, Aeron. That just means I've got a fifty-fifty chance of having a super bad eternity. There's not exactly a precedent for me!"

Leif just squeezed me.

"Yes, there is. You were an innocent victim in all this. You aren't going to Hell just because of your father and grandfather. You've helped save the world, Speedy. I think you've earned it, even without the angel blood."

"But you don't know for sure."

Dice just popped his toothpick out his mouth and smirked at me.

"I'd bet every single ounce of street cred I've earned stealing all the bombs on it."

Well, shit. Dice had a *lot* of street cred all over the fucking world for that, and I knew he liked that. He had a bit of a thankless job, and he had people thanking him that respected him. He wouldn't have said that unless he meant it.

Aeron kissed my hand.

"I'd bet my grace on it."

Well, wasn't Aeron trying to reassure me as blasphemously as possible? But he was looking at me like he was earnest. That was all his power. It was how the world hadn't ended so far. He was willing to offend God by telling me he'd risk it just to reassure me.

"You know I'm smart, right?" Leif said.

"Well, yeah. You're probably the smartest fucking person I've ever met."

"Then if you won't believe us about your mother, then trust us when we tell you that you'll build a ton of Heaven points stopping Satan from rising."

"Sorry, guys. I've just never given much thought to where I end up when I die, and then you dropped that on me. I guess stopping the end of the world would level the playing field."

Dice popped his toothpick in his mouth.

"Are you still mad at us?"

"I guess not, but try not to laugh when I ask questions anymore."

"Want to go blow off some steam and kill some of your father's people?"

"Totally."

Twenty-Three

I really wish I had more time to process all the shit that had been thrown my way since I woke up from that coma, but that was something that just wasn't available to me. I would have taken five more minutes to deal with my immortal soul, but Beavis and Butthead were in New Jersey dragging zombies, so we had to kill them.

In addition to having to deal with everything getting thrown at me in short amounts of time, I'd also become totally okay with killing. Before I got kidnapped, I couldn't even watch those ASPCA commercials about abused animals without ugly crying. Seriously, I teared up and donating every single time one came on.

But Leonard and this random Bubba? I didn't even bat an eye. My father told them to attack an entire state and kidnap me, and they just did it. With so little people left in the world, most sane people would question letting zombies eat an entire state and risking their lives to bring me back. I knew it was some sort of Nephilim superpower to inspire that kind of devotion, but seriously? Why were so many people willing to commit genocide for him.

Yeah, I had no problem killing people like that. It would save countless lives in the end. Dice had a location, and I just needed to trust them. I'd seen Aeron in action. Dice made a toy with Leif's serum in it. We could do this. Dice had a location. We just needed to get there.

"We're going to have to get there the angel way, Speedy. Is that okay?" Aeron said.

I fucking loved him for asking first. I nodded and wrapped my hands around his neck. My happiness at Aeron asking me soon faded when I realized he zapped me on top of a fucking moving RV with a prominent speaker on top with Leonard giving some sort of deranged sermon to the zombies. It had the Rage Heads riled up. They were following the RV and letting out those awful wails calling more of them.

All of the angels had their wings out for balance, and I couldn't even appreciate how sexy that was because it terrified me. Their wings were blocking my view of exactly how many zombies were surrounding us, but I could hear them, and I think that made it worse. I held onto Aeron and buried my face in his chest.

"If you drop me into those zombies, I swear I'll never have an orgy with you again."

"I got you, Speedy. Dice, can you get rid of those things?"

I heard Leif let out this little squeal like we weren't on top of a moving RV.

"I'm so excited to see my serum in action on the field."

"I just want to play with my new toy."

I was dating psychos. Psycho angels who thought this was fun. Newsflash, I was not having fun. Especially when whoever was driving the RV realized there was something up top and was trying to swerve it in this crowd of zombies. I just shrieked and clutched Aeron.

"Do you have this handled?" Aeron yelled.

"Oh, yeah," Dice said.

"I'm getting Ariel off the top of this RV and handling Beavis and Butthead. Speedy, want to get off the top of this RV?"

I didn't care where he was zapping me as long as it was off the top of a moving vehicle. I nodded, and, in an instant, we were fucking *inside* the RV. We were right behind the front seats. Leonard and Bubba jumped, and the entire RV swerved again. I could hear the thump of bodies as it ran over Rage Heads before it came to a stop. Aeron shoved me behind him and rested his arms on the headrest.

"Didn't anyone tell you zombie guts can totally ruin an engine before you decided on this whole road trip?"

"What the fuck, Leonard?" Bubba shrieked.

"It's an agent of Satan! Kill him!"

I know this spare Bubba was supposed to be along for protection, but he was totally freaking out we just appeared in the back of his RV. He was cowering in his bucket seat and just shrieking. Leonard was trying to get his gun from him to get rid of Aeron, but Bubba wouldn't let go.

Aeron was definitely insane, because he joined the fight for the gun. He quickly ripped it away from both of them and handed it to me like I knew how to use it and wasn't holding Smurfette. Even with zombies, Nazis, and random Bubbas trying to kill us, I still didn't like guns, but I definitely didn't want Leonard to have it. I wasn't worried about Bubba. He was now openly weeping. If my father had spare Bubbas lying around, he sure picked a bad one for wiping out Florida.

Aeron grabbed both of them by the collar and hauled them to the back of the RV. There wasn't a ton of room back here. There were two mattresses on the floor, and the rest of the space was full of food and gas cans. I definitely didn't want anyone shooting that gun in here with all this gas, but I had nowhere to put it since the whole interior of the RV had been gutted for this road trip.

Aeron was holding Leonard and Bubba up by their necks. I think Leonard was trying to perform an exorcism, and Bubba now had a wet spot on the front of his trousers.

"Which one did you want?" Aeron said, giving them a little shake.

"Oh, please don't kill me!" Bubba shrieked.

"Agent of Satan, I command you to leave this host!"

Aeron just sort of heaved Leonard into the gas cans.

"That is *so* not how you perform an exorcism, you twit. Do you mind if I take Leonard, Speedy?"

"Only if you promise to show him exactly how wrong he was helping Isaiah. I know it's too small in here for your wings, but improvise."

"Oh, they can make an appearance. Can you handle Beavis?"

Bubba was in the corner, rocking himself and crying. I think he shat himself too because I could smell it over the gasoline. All of the people I'd killed so far had been armed and trying to hurt me. I knew Bubba came along to kill everyone in Florida and help kidnap me, but he wasn't a threat right now. He'd soiled himself, and he was weeping way more than I ever did since I woke up from that coma.

I nudged Bubba with my toe, and he let out this

tremendous shriek. Aeron must have gotten all wingy and glowy and dropped the bomb about Isaiah because now Leonard was blubbering and asking for forgiveness. Aeron didn't let that go on for every long. I heard a squishing noise, and Leonard stopped talking. His head rolled straight into my foot. I kicked it away.

Aeron walked over with his bloody sword and looked down at Bubba.

"Why is this one still making that awful noise?"

"He's *crying*. I'm having a hard time smashing his head in. He's just an extra Bubba."

Aeron stabbed him in the chest with his sword. Blood bubbled out his mouth, and he slumped over dead.

"Yeah, he's pathetic, and he was expendable to your father, but if he was willing to come here and wipe out everyone in Florida and kidnap a girl, he's probably gotten up to some awful shit since the apocalypse started. We can't take those kinds of people in Florida, and we can't exactly send him back to Isaiah. If we let him go, he's not going to have some new lease on life because we appeared in the back of this RV."

"Are random Bubbas the red shirts of the apocalypse? Does my father have a bunch of Bubbas to spare?"

Aeron grabbed me and kissed me.

"I love that you randomly remembered the red shirts. Are you okay going back on the top of the RV now that it's not moving?"

I realized I couldn't hear wailing anymore. It was totally silent inside the RV. I could still hear them over Bubba and Leonard for a little while, but I couldn't hear a single sound anymore. I was curious about what was going on outside. I grabbed Aeron and told him I was okay with being out there now.

Leif and Dice weren't on top of the RV anymore. Where the fuck were they? I looked around in a panic. All the Rage Heads that had been following the RV were definitely dead for good this time. Leif's serum had not only killed them, but their bodies were slowly turning black on the ground.

"Where are they?" I demanded.

If there was ever a time for angel radio to happen, it was when Dice and Leif were missing, and corpses surrounded us.

Aeron pointed in the distance. I could see a Costco about fifty feet from the road.

"Looking for supplies. You don't think we're going to let this RV full of gas and food go to waste, do you?"

"We're going to drive back to Florida?"

"Between the three of us, we can carry it back, but you'll have to ride inside. Is that okay? I suppose you could hop on my back, but you'd be more comfortable sitting inside the RV."

I placed my finger over his lips because I knew he was about to babble.

"It's fine. Should we help them clear Costco of Rage Heads?"

"Leonard and Bubba drew them out with those speakers, and now they are all dead. New Jersey was a hot zone for the Rage Mutation. As far as we know, everyone that didn't turn left the state. Leonard and Bubba didn't just drive through here because it was on the way. There are no settlements here because everyone is dead, a Rage Head or they fled the state.

"Dice has enough of Leif's serum to clear what we can, but we need those devices they are working on in Florida to make it a safe place to live. I wouldn't feel bad about Leonard or that Bubba. Leonard helped do this, and Bubba profited off it in some way, or your father wouldn't have even known his name.".

I could see black corpses all over the place, and there were two dead men in the RV. I couldn't hear any Rage Heads wailing, but I still felt super exposed standing there on top of this RV even if no one was out there with a gun to take a potshot at me.

"Can we go to Costco? I'd feel safer with something to do. It feels weird standing here with all these dead bodies."

"Do you want to go the angel way or walk through the corpses?"

"Ew. The angel way. This is my only pair of boots."

"Maybe we can find you some more boots in Costco."

The apocalypse was so not the time to moan about how Costco probably didn't carry steel toe, knee-high combat boots, or lacy thongs. I'd be happy if I could grab some seriously expired deodorant, toothpaste, and dental floss. I'd been brushing my teeth with homemade toothpaste when I could get it, but I would watch Aeron kill Bubba again to brush my teeth with something minty with no grit.

Aeron zapped us to Costco, and it was just eerie. It felt like centuries had passed since I was in a ghost town raiding stores for supplies. I had gotten spoiled with the settlements I'd been in so far. Costco was dark. Most of the food had long been rotted, but the smell of it was still in the air.

Not only did angels have those handy angel pockets, but Aeron was his own personal flashlight and could light up the area around him. I poked him in the chest.

"Hey, glow-worm. Can I do that? There are some personal shopping items I'd like to find."

Aeron cocked an eyebrow at me.

"I know you haven't gone through that massive box of tampons you shoved in my face like they were solid gold."

"Tampons are *not* a luxury item and shouldn't be taxed as such. No one asked our opinion about having to bleed once a month, and I swear to God if you say anything about Eve and that apple, I'll castrate you."

Aeron held up his hands.

"I wasn't. I can tell you for a fact they consulted no woman on that. If you can make the lights go out, I'm pretty sure you can glow a little to light your way. I just don't know how to teach you. We're usually having sex when you cause a power outage, but this place stinks, and there's dirt everywhere. Maybe we can find the mattress section."

"We aren't fucking in Costco, Aeron."

"Are you sure? It could be kind of kinky."

"No way. I have to draw the line somewhere, and a stinky Costco isn't sexy. What do you do when you glow?"

"I channel my rage in my belly and let it out in little pieces unless I need to let it all out and kill people."

"I have rage."

"I know. You threaten me with it a lot. You should use it for something other than threatening to cut off my dick or not having orgies."

"How do you channel your rage like that?"

"I run through everything that has ever pissed me off until I'm in a foul mood. It's easy because it always hits you right in the gut. You just need to learn how to let it out in bits and pieces after that. I don't think you can kill anyone like we can, but you can stun and light your way.

You could use it against Isaiah instead of just shopping for tampons at Costco."

I was already running through every grievance I had with my father. I remembered those guys in Mexico that cut me and wanted to rape me. I even managed to remember my rivals on the roller derby circuit and the softball teams we always wanted to beat.

I could feel this intense feeling in my gut that I knew if I let it out, I was going to destroy something. I tried to just let out a little, even if this feeling was totally overwhelming, and I thought I was going to explode and get my insides all over this haunted Costco.

I really should have had my eyes open to see if this was working, but this was kind of like a night where the softball team hit up Taco Bell at midnight, and the night didn't end there. We were crass, rude, and vulgar, but we held in our farts because we were still *girls*. This was like four hours and several rounds of beer after Taco Bell level of trying to hold it in. How the hell did my angels even do this?

"Focus on your breathing, Ariel," Aeron said. "Just let out a little bit with each breath, then try to turn it off."

Oh, sure. Easy for him to say. I just ran through every little thing that had ever pissed me off, and now I needed a place to put it. Like Taco Bell, you couldn't just let it rip, or you might end up with a surprise.

I felt Aeron wrap his arms around my waist and press his chest to my back.

"I got you, Speedy. You can do this. I know it must feel totally overwhelming the first time. Breathe in with me. Now, let it out slowly and just let a trickle out. Good! Now, do it again and let out just a little bit more—one more time. Now, I want you to take everything you're feeling and tell it to just go away. Tell yourself to hold and focus on your happy memories. Open your eyes now, Speedy. You got this."

I cracked my eye open, and Costco was a lot brighter. I was fucking *glowing*. What a neat trick.

Aeron kissed the top of my head.

"Watch out for stray Rage Heads and go find you a Costco sized box of tampons, Speedy."

I started to wander off, totally jizzed I was fucking glowing. I knew what I wanted, but I wouldn't have been mad about finding a Costco sized box of tampons either.

TWENTY-FOUR

Since I slept through it, I guess I hadn't considered the sheer magnitude of the Rage Mutation. I'd seen the ghost towns, and zombies had surrounded me, but walking through this Costco just made it real. All the food was rotten, but the shelves were pretty much still stocked.

It was like everyone in New Jersey just turned, died, or left the state in such a hurry, there was an entire Costco full of supplies still left. They had abandoned New Jersey. No one tried to come here to clear out the Rage Heads and forage for supplies either. It was like every single state that surrounded it recognized the Rage Heads now owned this state, and they left them to it, even if there were a ton of supplies in just this store alone.

I ran into Leif at the pharmacy. That was where I went first because the rest of the shelves seemed full on my way back. I seriously thought I was going to start openly weeping when I saw tubes of toothpaste, mouthwash, and toothbrushes. I didn't care how expired they were, I grabbed a four-pack of deodorant, ripped it open, and applied it.

I had running water at the hotel and handmade soap, but most of the deodorant in Florida was gone, and I felt ripe by the time we went home, and I had to take another shower. I was hugging the deodorant display when Leif came running out of the pharmacy like a kid in a candy store.

"Can you believe this shit? This pharmacy still has all the good stuff."

"Leif, it's seriously shitty that all this is still here. That means everyone is dead and couldn't get this stuff. But everything here could seriously help the people in Florida, and it's not going to fit in that RV. I want things so I can brush my teeth and not stink, but there are medication, shelf-stable foods, and clothes in here that people could use."

Leif just pulled me into a hug.

"Our horses can carry a lot, and what do you like to call it? Angel pockets? Aeron will have to do most of the work since Dice and I are working on vaccines and the Rage Head problem, but all of this will get brought back to Florida."

"If I'm glowing, can I do the whole angel pocket thing?"

"I have no idea, Ariel. You're more angel than any Nephilim that came before you. None of us know exactly what you can and can't do."

"If I get fucked out of angel pockets like I did pockets in women's clothes, I'm going to get upset, Leif."

Leif squeezed me and kissed the top of my head.

"I do love you, Speedy. Even if you don't end up having angel pockets. I've already started moving some of the pharmacy back to an empty room at the hotel. I'd move it to my lab, but people should still be there working, and they'll freak out if opiates start randomly appearing."

"Some bad shit must have gone down in New Jersey if no one took the opiates. I know if I wasn't in a coma and my neighbors started eating people, I'd want to get a little high before I properly dealt with that shit."

"Um, these are for pain, not recreational purposes, Speedy."

"I don't mess with opiates, but I sure do miss Miss Mabel's weed stash. She always managed to find the good stuff."

Leif just laughed.

"Ask Dice. He probably knows who is growing in Florida, but seeing as how no one has offered at any of the gatherings, they might not share their stash."

I threw up my hands.

"That's the whole point of having a stash! It's just sad smoking up alone. Everyone knows it's puff, puff, give. What kind of apocalypse is this that people are hoarding weed? It's not like the cops are going to bust you because it's illegal in your state anymore. Can we do that when we rebuild the world? Can we make pot legal everywhere?"

"Baby steps, Ariel. We need to get everything out of this Costco before we worry about you being a pothead."

"Can I help? How do I figure out if I got angel pockets?"

I *really* wanted the angel pockets. I looked everywhere for uniform pants with pockets for my softball team, so I could pop a stick of gum when an inning started getting long. Newsflash, I couldn't find them *anywhere*. If I wanted pockets I could actually put things in, I had to buy men's pants. Angel pockets could solve *everything* when it came to storing shit I didn't want to carry.

"It's...I'm not sure how to teach this. You picture a space, then you just reach into it and move something in or out. It's all about intent. You have to have a firm picture in your head. Can you move your haul back to Dice's room?"

The angels looked so much cooler when they did this. I'm sure I looked constipated as I focused on the hotel room. The picture was about as straightforward as it was going to get. I grabbed as many tubes of deodorant as I could and thrust my hands out. And...nothing.

"Do I need to say a magic word? I've read all the Harry Potter books, and I self-identify as a mage in Dungeons and Dragons."

"I play as a cleric. If I knew you were into it, I would have searched a house and brought it back to my lab. Dice and Aeron think it's a nerd game. I think it's the only game Asher will actually participate in. He's an assassin."

"An angel is playing Dungeons and Dragons as an assassin?"

"Asher is a complicated guy. You don't need a magic word unless it helps you focus. It couldn't hurt. We all have unique powers, Ariel. I know you are watching us and wondering if you can do everything we can do, but no other angel can do some of the things we can do because they weren't created like us. Seeing the future is pretty fucking nifty, and none of us can do that. I'd give my left nut to be able to draw the future. Even if you can't do angel pockets, you're still pretty fucking powerful."

"Yeah, but I can't seem to get some fucking pockets no matter what I do," I moaned.

Leif gently took the deodorant from me and disappeared it into the hotel.

"You can use ours. What else do you want here?"

"Leif, the medication. That pharmacy is way more important than toiletries."

"Go grab a shopping cart from up front and load it up with what you want. I'll move the whole thing to the hotel room."

"Do you want me to grab you anything?"

"Clean boxers, and if they have any Twizzlers in here, I want some."

The Horseman of Pestilence created a vaccine and a kill serum. If he wanted clean underwear and some candy, I'd glow my way through this entire store until I found it. It bummed me I didn't have the whole angel pocket thing, but fuck. We killed Leonard, an extra Bubba, New Jersey had a lot fewer zombies, and we had an entire Costco to bring back to Florida.

Maybe I could make pockets happen in women's clothing when we rebuilt the world.

TWENTY-FIVE

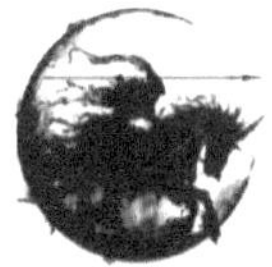

We all had jobs now. I was still painting, but Dice was working with the bombs, Leif was in his lab, and Aeron and I were emptying that Costco and ridding New Jersey of zombies. Dice gave both of us some sort of aerosol contraption that shot a grenade of Leif's serum. Aeron would zap us to New Jersey, and we would shoot it into heavily populated areas, then raid the Costco.

I was in the RV the first time this serum saw a horde of zombies, but now that I was getting to use it, I really appreciated Leif's genius. It was almost instant. Zombies would start dropping dead and turning black, and it made the air smell like Christmas because of the mistletoe. It was weird that zombie killing serums smelled that fucking good, but I just went with it because it made the Rage Heads nice and dead.

I knew Meremoth was Aeron's horse, but there was a red horse, a black horse, and a white horse at the Costco warehouse, helping us bring supplies back to Florida. The black horse was Leif's, the red one belonged to Dice, and the white horse was Asher's horse. I knew they were angel horses, but I swear, all of them were fucking with me when I tried to help load things in their saddlebags.

They were perfectly still when Aeron approached them, but when it was me, all four of them would stomp their hooves and toss their heads. I'd seen Aeron's horse in action, and I didn't want my death to be by horse, even if they were supposed to be on our side.

"Why do all these horses hate me?" I asked as I slid a pack of snacks in the saddlebag and jumped back. "I thought you said your horses were different than chickens?"

"Don't compare my horse to chickens, Ariel. You make them nervous because you're afraid of them. If you'd relax, so would they. They are worried your fear is going to get the best of you, and you'll try to hurt them."

"I'd never hurt an animal. I didn't even hurt those evil chickens back in Florida. I just ran. If your horse gets the urge to murder again, I'm running straight the fuck out of this Costco."

"Would it make you feel better if I told you our horses can tell the good guys from the bad and only kill the bad guys? Have you ever seen Meremoth kill anyone who wasn't trying to kill us?"

"No, but he killed them *with me on his back.*"

"Where else would you be when Rage Heads surround us? Honestly, there's no safer place to be. Meremoth has seen me through all kinds of war and death, and he's never thrown me once. He's kept me safe. Wait here."

Aeron disappeared into the Costco and left me alone with four huge murder horses that didn't like me. I gave them a wide berth. Aeron said they were scared all five foot eight inches of me was going to hurt them, but how could I possibly hurt an angel horse, even if I was okay with hurting animals?

I had all this bravado when it came to Nazis, zombies, and random Bubbas, but those horses could kill me in so many different ways, even if we were supposed to be on the same side.

Aeron came back like he'd just won the lottery and was holding something behind his back. Knowing him, he'd found a huge Costco sized stash of condoms or lube. I had no idea what he was doing when he produced a bag of sugar. I hope he knew I wasn't one of those girlfriends who was going to bake for him. I made a mean pot brownie, but I only baked if I was getting baked.

"Hold out your hand, Speedy."

I didn't know what he was doing, but I knew he was trying to show me something, and he wasn't laughing at me for not understanding this time. Aeron reached into the bag and placed a few sugar cubes in my hand.

"I'm glad we haven't gotten to this aisle yet because you are going to make friends with my horse, Speedy. I can't have my girl and my steed afraid of each other."

"I have way more reasons to be afraid of your horse than he does of me, Aeron."

"You and Meremoth got off on the wrong foot, and you didn't get a proper introduction because I couldn't tell you the truth when you first got on his back. You know all of us except Asher. It's time you got to know our horses. Stand totally still, don't say anything, and hold out your hand. Let him come to you."

I didn't know the first thing about horses. I was never one of those kids that wanted a pony growing up. I had bigger things to worry about. I had no idea how I was going to bribe a murder horse with sugar, but if I was going to date three of the Four Horsemen, I really needed to get over my shit with their horses. Maybe they were really nice murder horses.

Meremoth was eyeing my hand and let out this massive snort. In fact, all four horses had zeroed in on the sugar. Great, I was going to get murdered by four horses over some Costco brand sugar. I took a step back right into Aeron's chest.

"Easy, Speedy. You're making them nervous."

"Yeah, we have that in common right now."

"They won't hurt you. You have something they want. Let them come to you and get to know you."

"Why don't we find a coffee machine and some coffee and give them some caffeine too? Do we really want to give the murder horses sugar? That doesn't go down well with toddlers."

"We're giving them their favorite treat, and they will be wonderful. You've trusted me with a lot of shit, Ariel. Trust me about this."

"If your horse kills me, I'm going to haunt you for eternity, Aeron, and I'm going to be one of those mean ghosts that hides all your chargers and changes the television station right at the last ten minutes of a season finale."

"Ghosts aren't real, Speedy. Now, just relax."

Aeron pressed himself against my back and wrapped his arms around my waist. I felt much better about this with him right there. Hopefully, the horses wouldn't flip their shit with him touching me. I could do this.

I focused on the horses. I hadn't realized how beautiful they were now that I was just staring at them. They were so shiny and muscular. Meremoth met my eyes. I'd seen his eyes turn red, and I swear, he winked at me sometimes, but now that I was really looking at him, there was this preternatural intelligence in his eyes. It was the same for all four horses.

I found myself lost in those eyes and much less afraid of them as they started taking tentative steps towards me. These horses really were as nervous around me as I was around them. I wanted to get past this because I felt like shit I was spooking something so beautiful, even if they had given me a reason to be afraid of them.

I started making cooing noises. I *wanted* them to come closer now. I wanted at least one of these horses to take sugar from my hand. I didn't like being afraid of anything, and I wanted to get over my shit about this.

They started moving closer, and soon, I was surrounded by four massive horses, but I was less afraid of them than before. Meremoth's snout felt like satin in my palm as he gently ate the sugar. He didn't even bite me. The other three horses were checking my hair and my clothes for more sugar. It tickled, and I couldn't help laughing.

"Do you have some more of that sugar?" I asked Aeron as the red horse nuzzled my neck.

"Of course."

The horses were clearly intelligent because they weren't fighting each other over the sugar, even if they clearly liked it and wanted it. They were still nudging my neck and hair, but it was more like they were trying to caress me instead of getting me to hurry up with the sugar.

I managed to get sugar to all the horses and was loving every minute of this when Aeron kissed the top of my head.

"You've given them one of their favorite things. Why

don't you try petting their necks? Meremoth has a sweet spot right where his neck meets his shoulder, and the rest of the horses love it too."

I walked forward and started stroking the horse's necks. I couldn't call them murder horses anymore. Sure, they killed things pretty damned well, but they were just so sweet right now.

"Angel horses like sugar and pets?"

"They also like Guinness and eggs."

"You get your horse drunk? Aeron! That's worse than a sugared-up horse."

"Angel horses have a very specific diet. They get hay and grass, but we also supplement their diets to make them stronger. You'll find regular horses get a lot of the same things. You know I'd never hurt an animal, right? None of us would. We spoil Meremoth and the rest of our horses rotten. The reason they don't really stay with us here until we call them is that they have this epic stable where they are much more comfortable up in Heaven. Some people work there when we are on Earth who can handle their food and giving them a proper rub down at night."

"I'm glad we did this. Your horses are actually pretty cool."

"Want to go for a ride?"

I actually did, but all the horses had their saddlebags half full, and we spent the time we needed to get these supplies back to Florida for me to get over my fear of horses. I stroked Meremoth's soft mane.

"Tomorrow, yeah? We still need to get these supplies back, and the horses are loaded down."

Aeron grabbed me and kissed me.

"Have I ever told you how sexy you are sitting astride my steed?"

"I will admit to not being that comfortable on your horse before, but totally checking your ass out when you sat on him before. And I did like sitting there with you behind me."

"You'd better stop talking like that, or I'm going to find the mattress section."

"Where are we on moving things here?"

"We're still on the snack aisle. After we got everything out of the pharmacy, everyone wanted the junk food. We've still got half an aisle to go."

I grabbed Aeron and kissed him.

"Your wings are better than an operating forklift and sexy to watch."

"Mattress section?"

"Snack aisle, Aeron. People are counting on us."

Aeron ran his fingers through his hair.

"Doritos for all. Let's get back to work, Speedy."

Twenty-Six

I was so focused on getting everything out of that Costco and painting what I could remember that time seemed to slip by. We'd hardly put a dent in the shelves. Some lousy shit must have gone down in New Jersey because no one touched this Costco. If I had been awake when all this started, Costco probably would have been one of my top five picks to hole up in until I had no choice to leave.

No one had that chance here. There was no evidence someone had been squatting here. There were zero signs of life anywhere we went in New Jersey, but there was a shit ton of Rage Heads Aeron, and I were making dead for good.

I was back at Costco with Aeron. We'd managed to bring Doritos, chocolate, and Skittles to the masses in Florida and took requests for what was next. People wanted what was on the coffee aisle next. I loved my junk food. *Loved it.* But I'd already grabbed some coffee for me. We had excellent food in Florida, but I needed my black coffee.

Dice scared the shit out of me when he appeared right behind me. I turned around to throw coffee in the shopping cart and ran face first into his bare chest because he could never be bothered with shirts. I grabbed one of his unicorn suspenders and popped it against his chest.

"What are you doing? You scared me."

"Aeron! Get your ass over here."

Aeron looked wholly irritated with Dice, but he came trotting over.

"You'd better have a good reason for being here instead of at your workshop, and I swear to our Father if you're here because of Speedy like you were in Mexico, I'm going to beat your ass all over this Costco."

"Save your rage, Death. Pilots all over the fucking world have working bombs to kill the zombies and not the little humans. I just need to get on the radio and try to convince them to stay inside when we are flying. That's going to be the hardest part. Remember that pandemic right before the Rage Mutation? Humans take it as an affront to their person if they are asked not to leave their house, so they don't die."

I didn't remember the Rage Mutation, but I remembered that pandemic. Softball season got canceled, and it wasn't safe to open the tattoo shop. I kept myself occupied drawing and visiting Miss Mabel with a fucking mask. I had an entire collection of adorable masks.

That was when it hit me. I was caught up in what I could remember that I didn't take in all of what Dice said. I threw my arms around his neck.

"You seriously did it?"

"Yeah. We're flying out in three days. Leif has everything he needs to vaccinate everyone in Florida now. We're going to vaccinate everyone, then bomb the entire world, but in a good way."

I might be just as crazy as Dice, but I wasn't questioning him and his bombs anymore. I'd seen Dice do some crazy shit with the material he had on hand. If he said he could bomb the entire world and only kill the bad things, I believed him.

"Do you love me, Ariel?" Dice asked.

"Yeah, why?"

"Because it would be kinky if you ride bitch in my plane while I'm wiping out several states of Rage Heads at once."

Oh, shit. How long did it take me before I wasn't terrified to ride bitch on Aeron's horse? I enjoyed it now, and Aeron was taking me on rides through New Jersey, but a plane dropping bombs? That was well out of my comfort zone.

"I thought you were the *Horseman* of War, not a pilot. I didn't think you actually fought in wars. You just moved pieces and ended them."

Dice just kissed the top of my head.

"War, Conquest, and Death have all personally been on the front lines. Leif could fight too if he wanted to, but he's just so fucking smart. We always leave him to his microscopes and test tubes. I'd love to take you up on my plane. There's no danger. Your father can't shoot us out the air because I have all the pilots and all the bombs. Game, set, match. We drop the bombs, kill your father, then we can have our orgy next to his corpse."

I wrinkled my nose.

"That's not sexy, Dice. As much as it makes me nervous because I've never been on a plane before, I actually would find it sexy to ride bitch in your plane. Can I paint you all sexy and topless in your jet when this is over?"

"I'd be mad if you didn't. Can it be one of those jumbo-sized paintings? I like the idea of my hotness hanging in some museum after I get called back home."

"So, I can't hang that one in my bedroom as spank bank material?"

Dice grunted and nipped at my nose.

"You're dating the Horsemen of the Apocalypse, Speedy. What makes you think you'll have the energy to do that with us around?"

"Truer words have never been spoken, Dice," Aeron said. "Once we don't have to worry about stopping the Antichrist, I'm never going to let Ariel leave the bed."

"I still have to work, Aeron."

"Why? Leif doesn't just have a lab in Mexico. We have an estate there. It's just not in San Quintin where we were staying. We can grab Mabel, retire in Mexico, and live on the beach. You can paint to your heart's content."

"We still have to kill my father first," I pointed out.

I knew we had that whole painting I had done where we won, but decades before, I'd also painted a scenario where they lost. If my visions could change based on decisions, then anything could happen when we got to the Oval Office. I hadn't exactly done a new painting of an updated scenario of how that would go down.

Really, anything could happen, and I'd steeled myself for it. For now, I was actually excited to ride bitch in Dice's jet.

TWENTY-SEVEN

Disneyworld was bustling now that a vaccine was going to be administered, and the planes would go out soon. Aeron was still raiding the Costco with Dice, but Dice had a special request, and I felt like I should oblige him. He knew I had been drawing their horses and had met his horse. He wanted me to paint a stylized version of his horse, Arrio, on the side of his plane.

I hadn't ridden on Arrio, but I'd gotten to know him a little at Costco. Out of all the horses, he liked sugar the most. He also liked to bury his nose in my hair and nuzzle my neck.

I was happy to paint him on the side of Dice's plane. I had several sketches, and Dice refused to look at them and approve one. He wanted me to surprise him. Whichever one I picked, I knew it was going to have to be unique. None of the Horsemen had asked me to draw anything for them before, even though they were incredibly supportive and amazing about my art. It was more than just the fact that at any moment, I could draw the future, and it helped us. They buttered me up about my regular drawings too, and I loved them for that.

Dice had a can of old, red boat paint in his workshop. He gave it to me and left me in the hangar with all the planes with his baby. It didn't take long. I wasn't painting a highly detailed portrait of Arrio, but I did make it big and stylized. I wanted anyone who saw that plane to know it was Dice's.

While I was working on that, Leif and his team were vaccinating Florida while Dice and Aeron worked on pulling things from the shelves at Costco. It only took me one day to paint the horse, but Dice didn't want to see it until takeoff. He wanted it to be a surprise.

After I finished, I didn't know where I should be. I wandered over to Leif's set up where people were getting their vaccinations, but Leif had an entire team helping him. There were just as many people helping here as there were in Mexico. The only difference was Leif didn't have a massive stack of gifts behind him.

I was watching him from a distance when someone snuck up behind me and spoke.

"He's something, isn't he? We're celebrating the vaccine and the planes by slaughtering one of the cows. We're having burgers and barbeque. Jana and George are mass making buns, and we have plenty of veggies for toppings. Dice and Leif brought back some condiments from wherever y'all are finding all these supplies from."

We couldn't exactly tell anyone we were stealing supplies from a Costco way the fuck in New Jersey without people asking how we got there. Plenty of people in Mexico knew there was something supernatural and Leif and Aeron, but everyone here thought they were just really massive humans who knew their shit.

"I'd be there with them, but Dice asked me to paint his plane."

I realized it was Stephanie behind me, the lady who made that fantastic strawberry beer our first day. She was so sweet, and she was running a brewery out of one of the restaurants outside the theme park.

"I've seen you painting. You're amazing."

"Not as good as your beer."

Stephanie bowed her head.

"I'm debuting an apple ale tonight, and I've had some homemade whiskey aging in a barrel I was saving for the right occasion. This is definitely it. Dice says you'll all be leaving soon, and hopefully soon, there will be a new government working to rebuild."

I was so glad Dice didn't promise a definite. I was also glad no one here knew the President was my father because everyone here seemed to hate him. Some of the drawings were crude, but people were drawing him and using him for target practice with arrows. I didn't even have to ask. I knew they all had swords, but I'd bet money Dice taught people how to hunt with bows.

"That sounds amazing, Stephanie."

"So, are you with all three of them?"

I let out this little growl. Was she stepping in on my men? I'd hate to kill her because she made excellent beer, and I wanted some of that whiskey.

"Yes, I am. Why?"

"Woah, girl. I was just asking. They are cute, but I'm not going to step on your toes. Plenty of women wanted Dice, but after his friends showed up, he wouldn't take anyone for a lover, male or female. I guess he was waiting for you to get here."

Dice waited for me? I knew why Leif and Aeron did.

We'd gotten to know each other over chat, and we were technically dating. But Dice? I didn't particularly want to know about them, but I just assumed he'd taken lovers here before he got to Mexico and met me. That fucker waited. I was going to have to kiss him when I saw him again. Did he wait this entire time because of my painting?

"Dice seriously acted like a monk until I got here?"

Stephanie just laughed and tossed her hair over her shoulder.

"Much to the chagrin of every woman here. We didn't see him much. If he wasn't in his workshop, he was on his laptop looking for something. We never knew what it was, but when he found it, we had this gigantic party."

Me. I knew Dice was the one that finally found me. He threw a fucking party, even though he'd never even met me.

He might not let everyone see it, but the Horseman of War was a big softy.

Twenty-Eight

Aeron and I had a system at Costco, but Dice and Aeron appeared to have shopped for the best burgers and steak seasonings and condiments possible while I was off painting. I totally wasn't complaining. I made a graceful exit when it was time to slaughter the cow and focused on my artwork, but I was definitely enjoying the spoils now.

There were burgers and steaks at the cookout. There wasn't enough for everyone to get their preferred cut of meat, but when someone told me they saved me a steak, I shut up and thanked them.

The apple ale was terrific and so was the whiskey. The company was even better. I was trying to forget that in the morning, a lot of us would be boarding planes and dropping bombs. I didn't hear what Dice said on his radio show because he did it at Costco, but he seemed convinced most people would stay inside.

"I wish you were in my plane," Aeron grumped.

"Me too," Leif said.

"*All* of you can fly planes? What the shit?"

Leif just grinned at me.

"I don't usually get to because I'm in my lab, but I get to have my fun before we head to D.C. Since I've seen the serum in action, I know it'll work. I'll still have to work on getting the vaccination out to the rest of the US just in case there's still tainted water someone could come across, but I can play for now."

I grabbed his hand.

"I love it when you play. I want playtime when this is all over."

"You'll be lucky if you get to leave the bed when this is over," Aeron said.

"Tell me about your house in Mexico, Leif. Aeron was telling me about it."

Leif just shrugged.

"It's technically a house for all of us, but I was the one that had it built. There's a mother in law suite in the back, so you could bring Mabel if she wants to come."

Would she? I wanted my ever after with the Horsemen, but my one-bedroom apartment wouldn't hold all of us, and I didn't think I could live anywhere except next door to Miss Mabel. She'd like a mother in law cottage, but there were also things she would want.

"Miss Mabel is going to want a place to buy ingredients to cook and a pot hookup."

"I checked on the estate while I was working in the lab. Several families live there and take care of it. It's passed down like my lab. All of the families are safe, and there's a farm there. There's a village nearby that will have to rebuild before she can get groceries, and I actually have no idea about pot."

"I have some growing by the outhouse you refuse to

take out because you think it gives the property character. It's the good stuff, too," Dice said.

Leif smacked Dice on the back of the head.

"You planted pot on my property? What the fuck were you thinking?"

"That if I was going to be living in the same house as Aeron, I was going to need it."

"Dick," Aeron said.

"You know you love me."

"I love punching you in the face."

"Do we have to save that mother in law cottage for Mabel," Leif said. "Do you know how long I've been listening to these two bicker like an old married couple?"

I just laughed.

"Most married couples don't threaten to beat the shit out of each other."

Aeron just rolled his eyes.

"You should see Henry VIII and all his wives go at it. I won't even go to that part of Heaven."

"Henry the VIII ended up in Heaven? He killed so many of his wives!"

"Yeah, but he created an entire church. Brownie points," Leif said.

"This is never going to make sense to me. What about Hitler? Where did he end up?"

"Hell, totally. Dictators always end up there because they are never up to any good," Leif said.

"Who is up there that I would be totally shocked about?"

"Besides Henry VIII?" Dice said. "Loads of people shocked us. Heaven is a big place."

"Fess up, is there a Heaven for pets? The whole rainbow bridge thing?"

Leif kissed my hand.

"Your lost pets will be waiting for you when you get there."

"I wasn't allowed to have anything furry on my lease, but I did have a charming beta fish who would puff up when I changed clothes."

"Smart fish," Aeron grunted.

Leif looked far away.

"We could get a dog and a cat when we retired in Mexico. I've always wanted a pet. I think we should find a stray, rescue it, and tame it. I've always been big on animal rescue."

"And that's one of the many things I love about you."

Whatever happened in D.C., I really wanted to beat my father. Not only would we save the world, but I really wanted my lovely house in Mexico with pets and my Horsemen.

TWENTY-NINE

The day had arrived. We couldn't magically appear in the hangar, so we took the horses. The angels got into a minor spat over whose horse I was going to ride on, and Leif actually got involved this time. I thought all three of them were going to get in one of the famous fistfights I'd heard so much about. I ended up settling it by saying I'd been on Aeron's horse plenty of times, and I'd take Leif's horse on the way there and Dice's on the way back. They grumped, but they accepted it.

It was so lovely sitting on Leif's horse with his muscular arms wrapped around me. Leif's horse was more on the playful side, especially when he had sugar. He was always nipping at my ears in ways that were so ticklish.

The moment of truth had arrived. We were at the hangar. Everyone knew I was painting Dice's plane for him, and I couldn't wait for him to see it. His people couldn't either. They had thrown this massive tarp over the nose of the plane and tore it off with this gigantic flourish when he arrived.

Dice scooped me up and spun me around.

"It's beautiful. Will you tattoo this on my chest when this is over?"

"We should all have Ariel tattoo our horses on us. It'll be a bonding moment. Talking Asher into that is going to be an enormous pain in this ass, but it would be special," Leif said.

I tried not to think about Asher. He was still this massive mystery. I knew he didn't want to be with me, and I wasn't all that on board with having an orgy with him either. Still, I seemed to be collecting Horsemen at an alarming rate, and meeting Asher would probably be just as awkward as Dice because he knew about the painting.

Dice looked like he intended on flying the plane in leather trousers and kitten suspenders, but he wouldn't let me on his plane until I'd put a jumpsuit on over my clothes and had been strapped into a helmet. He handed me a headset, popped his helmet on, and hopped into the cockpit.

"Any last words?"

"Um, don't you need someone on the ground, making sure we don't all crash into each other?"

Why didn't I think of that before I hopped in the back of this plane? I knew Dice could handle himself, but what about all the other people out there flying?

Dice just chuckled and checked my seatbelt.

"Already handled. We've got a retired airport employee at the Orlando airport, and it has power. She's got us, and I've got you. You ready?"

"Yes," I squeaked.

This could only happen to me. Only I would have my first time in a fucking plane be a fighter jet driven by an angel to bomb Louisiana, Texas, and Arkansas. Seriously, if we got to retire in Mexico, I wanted a totally dull existence until I died after that. I wanted to play bingo with Miss Mabel and never have to deal with Antichrists and zombies ever again.

I squeezed my eyes shut when the engine roared to life. We had to wait our turn. Some of the people who were going as far as the West Coast and Mexico were leaving first. We weren't going far. Aeron was taking care of New York and the surrounding states, and Leif was handling the Midwest. They both left before us.

When it was finally our turn, I was gripping the armrest and shrieking curses as we took off down the runway, but once we were in the air, it wasn't so bad, even if it was loud.

"You good now, Speedy?"

"Much better."

"Did you know if you look to your left...the plane will tip over?"

"Dice!" I yelled, trying to swat at his helmet.

"Seriously, though. Look out the window. It's pretty."

I'd never been afraid of heights before, so this didn't bother me. Crashing the plane certainly did, but looking down below didn't. I could really see the devastation the last bombs had caused, but I could also see where nature was fighting back. Greenery was trying to grow again, even if it looked like some ancient trees had died.

I looked out the window and focused on the radio chatter during the flight. I had no idea what any of it meant, but it was mesmerizing. Someone was sitting at a booth in Orlando and controlling everyone. Fucking amazing. I didn't understand a single word out her mouth, but I was going to have to paint her something special for doing this.

It felt like Dice was slowing a bit.

"I'm going to be dropping here. This is the perfect, unpopulated spot for the aerosol to hit all three states."

It was so uneventful. Dice pressed a button, and the place shook a little. He turned us around, and we started flying home. It felt like something bigger should have happened. We dropped a bomb on three states, and all the zombies were going to die.

And nothing happened.

Did I even want it to? It made me feel better that my father was shit out of luck when it came to stopping us, but it also filled me with dread. The Rage Heads were supposed to be his soldiers in his war against Heaven. If all he did to stop us was Leonard and a random Bubba, did he have something even bigger planned when we came for him?

Because we were coming for him, and we were going to try to kill him. He didn't just piss off the Four Horsemen. He pissed me off too.

And I was coming for him.

Thirty

Dice was eerily silent when we got back. He didn't speak and just kept moving all this equipment out to the picnic tables. We had gotten started pretty early in the morning. I didn't have a watch, but the angels could tell time by the sun, and Leif informed me it was three in the morning.

It was now starting to get dark, and people were slowly trickling back in from their flights. We were eating leftover burgers, and there was more apple beer. No one was talking, and I had no idea why. Did something go wrong that I didn't know about?

Dice finally hopped on the picnic table. He had his MP3 player out and a small headset on.

"People of the United States. Florida has brought you a gift. You should be able to leave your houses now, and you'll notice the Rage Heads are now dead. Burn them, don't bury them. But be smart about it. Don't cause fire damage. We are about to move into the process of rebuilding the world.

"We've been through some shit. We've all lost people.

It's time to move forward. In a few weeks, we will elect a new government and remaking the world. But now we just celebrate. Mourn your dead. Give them a proper rest.

"We're all scattered now. Some of us are no longer in our home states. We don't talk to our neighbors anymore, and I want that to change. If you have a radio, I want to hear your story. We all do. The entire country wants to hear from you. This is more than just my music. We have a shared experience. If you're hearing this and you have a way to talk back to us, do it. Tell us your story. Tell us about the people you lost. This is all we have now. We are our stories."

Dice just hopped off the table, plugged his MP3 player into his contraption, and took a bite out of his burger. We all just waited. Was someone going to talk to us? Would I actually hear from someone who wasn't in a state I'd already been to?

"Hello?" a male voice said.

"Hello. What's your name, friend?"

"Davis."

"Where are you from, Davis?"

"New Jersey."

Oh, shit. A living person from New Jersey after everything I saw there?

"Some nasty shit went down in New Jersey, Davis. Tell us your story. How did you survive?"

I heard Davis's breath hitch.

"We were visiting family in Georgia when the Rage Mutation hit. We tried calling our family and neighbors back home, but we got no answer. We wanted to go home, but they blocked all the roads with traffic, and the news cut out shortly after that. One of my friends back in Newark does radio as a hobby, but I couldn't raise him either. We've gotten no news from New Jersey. Do you know what happened?"

"This all started because of tainted water, Davis. Armilus did this on purpose. New Jersey got hit pretty hard by the Rage Mutation, as did several other states who totally adopted their water supplement. If you didn't turn, it means you avoided the tainted water, or you have a certain blood type. We will deliver a vaccine soon in case there is any of the water left."

"Who *are* you? None of the governments have been able to fix this so far. How did some random man in Florida?"

I bit my fist. I was sure Dice, Aeron, and Leif just *loved* being referred to as some rando in Florida. I was trying so hard not to giggle.

"I didn't do this alone, Davis. We *all* did this. I had help from all over the country. Several states helped with this, and Mexico was where the vaccine was produced. We're going to fix the world. Tell me, Davis. Are you still in Georgia?"

"My brother-in-law has a house with one of those fallout shelters. We've been down here for years. We came down when war broke out. We're starting to run low on rations, so your help came just in time."

"Whereabouts in Georgia are you, Davis?" Aeron asked.

"The outer Macon area."

"All the Rage Heads out that way are dead now, but you still have to worry about some people who didn't turn. There's a lot of disorder in Atlanta right now."

A group of men stepped forward.

"We can bring a truck and go get them until we settle

things. We have enough gas, and Georgia isn't too far away."

"No!" Davis said. "If there are bad people out there, they could have a radio and hear this. They'll set an ambush."

"He's right," Dice said. "How soon will you run out of supplies, Davis?"

"Maybe a month."

"Can you hang tight another two weeks? By then, my people will have handled some things, and my team can personally bring you some supplies and deal with the riffraff."

"Oh, thank you! My battery is about to die, but I've been listening to your show every day."

"Take care, Davis. We're coming."

Now that Dice and Aeron had set the scene for personally helping people, I expected people to blow up the airwaves wanting food and help. But the line went silent until I heard a laugh I never wanted to hear again.

"Well, aren't you just so fucking helpful? Are all four of you here this time? I know you have Ariel," Isaiah said.

I guess now that Dice had opened up the airways, anyone could use them. It felt like someone had dumped ice water over my head, but I wasn't afraid. I was furious. I wanted to jump through that radio and strangle him.

My gentle Leif just started laughing like a madman.

"Oh yeah. We're all here, and we're coming for you. We got rid of your little pets, Isaiah. America, do you know who was pulling strings at Armilus and created the Rage Heads? Your fucking president!"

What was Leif doing? He was going to cause riots. Aeron had gone around spreading the word about the tainted water, but I didn't think anyone knew Isaiah was the mastermind behind it all.

"The rantings of a terrorist!" Isaiah said. "These men kidnapped my daughter, and they were the ones who created the Rage Mutation."

Did Isaiah think they were keeping me in a little box, and I wasn't allowed to speak? I mean, I was sitting *right here.* And I was about to clear up some shit. If it meant an angry mob with pitchforks and torches took him out instead of me, the end goal was still the same. He would be good and dead.

"Hi, First Daughter here, and I can totally speak for myself. Isaiah experimented on me and terrorized me as a child. He kidnapped me again after I ran away and kept me in a coma at a research facility trying to find a way to make those of you that didn't turn Rage Heads too. I've got flash drives of the research, shit head. I've read the emails. Remember how pissed off you got about Hillary's emails? I've got yours, and when the internet comes back up, they are going to get plastered everywhere."

"America, can you see how evil these terrorists are? Do you see how they've groomed my own child against me? Do you see—"

"Hey, shit for brains!" I yelled, cutting him off. "If what I say isn't true, then why wasn't I mentioned during your campaign? If I was off missing getting groomed by terrorists, why didn't you make a fucking peep about it? If you knew the water caused the Rage Mutation and knew who caused it, why didn't you say *anything* on your radio show about it? You sent Nazis to Mexico because you knew they were working on a vaccine there, but you never warned a single damned person about the water."

"You're delusional, Ariel, and I'll be praying for you.

America, we do need to come together, but it's fighting these terrorists. You see what they've done to my own child. You can't trust that vaccine developed with a bunch of spics. You know we can't trust anything and anyone that comes out of Mexico. They bring crime here, and that vaccine is going to kill you. This has been their plan all along."

"You're such a racist fuck," I growled.

All of those people that didn't want to share their stories when Dice asked were chiming in now. I heard accents from all over the fucking country.

"If I had enough gas, I'd come to D.C. and waste a perfectly good bullet on you."

"You're going to burn in Hell for this. No one actually voted for you. You just seized the throne, and I hate your radio briefs. You say nothing important. All you do is stoke hate."

"Where are the terrorists? I'm not taking that vaccine. Everyone who is woke knows they use vaccines to sterilize you or microchip you. Like I'd ever trust a vaccine out of Mexico. Tell me where they are, and I'll end this myself."

The radio was blowing up from both sides—people who could look at the evidence and see the Rage Heads were now dead because of the Horsemen where Isaiah hadn't lifted a finger to stop them or warn them about the water. Then there were the people who saw terrorists in anything unfamiliar and were willing to side with the Antichrist out of fear.

Dice cut that shit right off.

"We have proof of Isaiah's crimes, and they will be made public soon. Before another war breaks out, I'm ending this. Enjoy some fucking John Lennon."

Dice and his toys. He just swiped up on his MP3

player, and all the arguing stopped, and what must have been every single antiwar song John Lennon ever wrote started playing.

Dice gave us a grim look.

"Did you *have* to do that, Leif? We would have released that information after we killed him. You've just pissed off the entire country. I expect that shit from Aeron, but not from you."

"He was *taunting* us, Dice. He would have gone the terrorist route eventually because he knows we are coming. He knows his Rage Head army is dead, so he wants a wall of humans around him to stop us. I just leveled the playing field so they are after him too."

Don't ask me where this man came from, but I could just tell he was the missing Horseman I hadn't met yet when he stormed up to the picnic table and flopped down. He was the same size as the other angels, but his hair was pure white and way longer than the other Horsemen. He had it pulled back with a strip of leather.

He was dressed head to toe in black, and he had a black bandana around his neck like he pulled it up to disguise his face. He ran his hand down his face and glared at Leif. He totally ignored me.

"What the fuck are you thinking? All the militias Isaiah has gathered for personal security are riled up and swarming the White House. You know those people love a good terrorist story and have a problem with facts and evidence. They are ready to blow the head off of anyone who so much as farts in Isaiah's direction. Why didn't you just cut him off when he decided to make an appearance to taunt you? Wasn't that the entire point of your radio show? To silence him?"

I guess I was finally meeting the mysterious Asher,

who took one look at the shitshow going down in D.C. and decided to make an appearance in Florida. I hadn't officially met him. I was just sitting at the same table. He hadn't spoken to me and was acting like I didn't exist.

"You know how the Antichrists are, Asher. They are just like movie villains. I watch the same movies Aeron does, and I've got a history of Antichrists to go on. I was hoping if I let him talk a little, he'd drop something that would help us. Leif just got his panties in a twist and pissed off the entire country. But he is right, in a way. Isaiah would have known he's next and riled up his army of Bubbas."

"Well, we have to step up our plans because not everyone in D.C. and the surrounding areas are a part of his militia. Many people have radios there, and they heard that shit. We have to stop Isaiah before another war breaks out, and we *have* to get the proof of his crimes out, so those loyal to him stand down. I don't think you understand the sheer number of armed people outside the White House right now."

Aeron stood and ran his fingers through his hair.

"I haven't gotten to kill anything since Leonard and Bubba. Let's get back to the hotel so we can get to Asher's hole up in D.C."

I held out my hand. If he would not introduce himself, then I was.

"I'm Ariel. Or you can call me Speedy if you want."

Asher looked at my hand like I covered it in green baby shit and refused to take it.

"I'm aware. I think you should stay here."

Okay, the Horseman of Conquest was a bit of a dick, and who was he to bench me right at the end? I *needed* to see Isaiah die. Dice, Leif, and Aeron surrounded me.

"She's coming with us," Aeron growled.

"We can't leave her," Dice said.

"We can't have a Nephilim you're all fawning over with us while we take down the most dangerous Antichrist we've encountered so far!" Asher said.

Leif just slung his arm over my shoulder and smirked.

"She *has* to come. You know she's a Harbinger, and she's painted us in the White House twice now. Without her, we die. With her, we have a totally lovely orgy after we send Isaiah back to Hell."

Asher just scowled.

"Fine, but I'm not babysitting her. Let's go before more people die."

We started heading off to the hotel. The time had come to face my father and his militias, finally. I didn't blame Leif for getting mad and letting it slip that Isaiah was responsible for the Rage Mutation. We were about to kill the sitting President. He didn't get that seat legally, and he definitely abused his power. Still, even if people didn't like him, they got upset when you assassinated government officials, even if they were the Antichrist.

We would have had to get our proof out with angry mobs after us. Sure, Leif created different angry mobs, but at least it would make a little more sense to the more reasonable people in the population when we announced he was dead and tried to show them our proof.

Asher walked ahead of us while Leif, Aeron, and Dice stayed close to me and held my hand. This was it. Everything we had done so far to get to this point was paying off. People in several states had been vaccinated, and Rage Heads all over the world were dead. We just needed to kill the Antichrist, and I could retire in Mexico with my angels.

My heart was thumping in my chest, and my adrenaline was pumping. I was going to get my revenge for everything he had done to me and what he had done to the entire world. I was sure he had some ace up his sleeve, but I had all four Horsemen now.

Asher seemed to hate me and didn't want me to be there, but he had a vested interest in sending Isaiah back to Hell. Surely that would mean he wouldn't let me die at the White House, right? Asher was this big question mark, and he didn't seem like he wanted to get to know me.

So, why the fuck was he included in that painting I did? I pushed the painting aside. I didn't need to be thinking about orgies right now.

I was totally going to Tyrion Lannister my father, and I was here for it.

Afterword

So, I spent a lot of time in this series talking about Speedy's favorite book series, *Blood Feud*. I'm not sure when it's going to release, but I kind of actually want to make it happen. I've already made the cover. Evil vampire assassins that kill and fuck everything? It's 2020 and that's a total mood.

So, *Blood Feud* is totally going to happen, but probably not until next year because I have a lot of things on my plate to write for the next few months.